"I'm not   a   n   just a one hundred percent regular woman."

The words caused Drew's abdomen to contract. An air of awareness hung in the room like fog.

One hundred percent woman? Definitely.

Regular? No way.

His pulse deepened as an unexpected pull toward this woman gripped him. Not solely because of the easy, loving manner she had with his son, either, although that was definitely a plus. But aside from that, Lexy Cabrera was, quite frankly, stunning. She wore jeans and a red tank top that showed off tanned and super-toned arms and shoulders. She reminded him of an exotic Marilyn Monroe, all dark tumbled hair, slanted bedroom eyes and creamy cappuccino skin. Super sexy without even trying.

Yeah, Lexy was leaps and bounds beyond regular.

Dear Reader,

I've been the voice behind 9-1-1 for eight years, now, and certain calls reach out and imprint themselves on your soul. Usually those are from children, who are braver and more capable under pressure than we give them credit for.

So it is when Lexy answers a terrifying, life or death 9-1-1 call from six-year-old Ian Kimball. Afterward, Lexy knows heroic little Ian will always be in her heart, but she didn't expect his widowed father to find his way there, too.

She quickly realizes Drew Kimball is far more than simply a patient, or the new guy in town, or a sexy, eligible daddy. He's the one and only man who makes her contemplate risking her heart again.

For those who've followed Lexy through the first three Troublesome Gulch books and begged me not to forget about her (I never would!), I hope you find her healing path as satisfying as you did her friends'.

Wishing you health, safety and, of course, love,

Lynda

LEXY'S LITTLE MATCHMAKER

LYNDA SANDOVAL

SPECIAL EDITION

Published by Silhouette Books

America's Publisher of Contemporary Romance

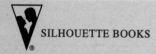 SILHOUETTE BOOKS
®

Recycling programs
for this product may
not exist in your area.

ISBN-13: 978-0-373-65460-4

LEXY'S LITTLE MATCHMAKER

Copyright © 2009 by Lynda Sandoval

Visit Silhouette Books at www.eHarlequin.com

Printed in U.S.A.

Books by Lynda Sandoval

Silhouette Special Edition

**And Then There Were Three #1605
*One Perfect Man #1620
*The Other Sister #1851
*Déjà You #1866
*You, and No Other #1877
†Her Favorite Holiday Gift #1934
*Lexy's Little Matchmaker #1978

**Logan's Legacy
*Return to Troublesome Gulch
†Back in Business

LYNDA SANDOVAL

is a former police officer who exchanged the excitement of that career for blissfully isolated days creating stories she hopes readers will love. Though she's also worked as a youth mental health and runaway crisis counselor, a television extra, a trade-show art salesperson, a European tour guide and a bookkeeper for an exotic bird and reptile company—among other weird jobs—Lynda's favorite career, by far, is writing books. In addition to romance, Lynda writes women's fiction and young adult novels, and in her spare time, she loves to travel, quilt, bid on eBay, hike, read and spend time with her dog. Lynda also works part-time as an emergency fire/medical dispatcher for the fire department. Readers are invited to visit Lynda on the Web at www.LyndaLynda.com, or to send mail with a SASE for reply to P.O. Box 1018, Conifer, CO 80433-1018.

For the brave little girl who called 9-1-1
and followed all my CPR instructions despite her fear.

Your grandpa will always be your guardian angel.

Chapter One

Drew crouched at the carved wooden sign with white-painted letters and clapped a hand on his son's slight shoulder, warm from the sun. "What's that say, pal?"

Ian studied the words, his bottom lip jutting out in concentration. The expression always reminded Drew of Gina. "Um...Deer Track Trailhead." He squinched his nose at his dad. "That's hard to say."

"Yeah, it's a tongue twister—" Drew stood, then ruffled Ian's golden hair "—but easy to remember, right? Deer Track?"

"Yep," Ian said. "Deers make tracks."

"That's a good way to think of it." Drew angled his chin down. "You won't forget if you repeat the name in your head three times, just like I taught you."

Ian squinted up at him and smiled. "I already did."

"Good boy." Drew lifted one arm and glanced at his wristwatch. "Ready for synchronization?"

Ian mimicked his father's action, focused on his plastic digital superhero watch. "Mine says 11:11 a.m."

Drew nodded once. "Mine, too."

"Okay, so we started hiking from the Deer Track Trailhead," Ian enunciated carefully, "at 11:11 a.m. You remember, too, Daddy. Just in case."

Drew smiled down at his son, his heart swelling. "That's right. The Kimball men can never be too prepared. You have your water bottle and energy bar?"

"It's all in here." Ian hooked his thumbs beneath the shoulder straps of his Batman backpack. He was in the midst of an extended superhero worship phase. Nothing could harm a superhero, after all. "And the special card I made for Mommy's in here, too."

It took all of Drew's will to keep the soul-cutting pain out of his expression. "That's my little man."

"I don't forget stuff."

"No, you sure don't. Let's get started. We have a long day ahead of us." Drew blinked up at the crackling sun. "Looks like it's going to be a hot one."

Ian slipped his hand into his father's. "Did you used to hike here when you were little, Daddy?"

"I did." Boy, that had been a lifetime ago. "With your grandpa."

"Cool," Ian said.

Their hiking boots crunched softly on the packed dirt as they ascended the path through the Rockies. All around them, summer wildflowers bloomed with riotous, multicolored abandon, and the soft breeze through the evergreens sang on the air like angels' whispers. Birds chattered in the trees, and the occasional chipmunk darted through the underbrush. In a word? Peaceful. And heartbreaking, but that was two words. This ritual, on this particular day— the anniversary of Gina's death—might be excruciating for Drew, but it was important.

For Ian.

Drew set aside his private pain and sucked it up. Ian peered up at the steep climb ahead of them. "I really think we'll be closer to her at the top of the mountain, Daddy." His voice had gone pensive, albeit determined.

After a moment to school his emotions, Drew smiled tightly at Ian. "Of course we will," he said, in a gentle tone. He felt the sudden need to fill up the silence with words that might make the whole thing easier. "See those clouds?" He pointed to a blindingly white thunderhead hanging in the deep turquoise Colorado sky.

"Yeah?"

"That's the part of heaven we can see from here on earth."

"Where Mommy is?"

"Yes." Drew cleared the catch from his throat. "And Mommy's always watching you from heaven, okay? Taking care of you."

"What about you?"

"Both of us, son. Every time you look at those clouds, think of her and believe."

Ian's wide-eyed stare remained fixed on the fluffy cloud. "We *will* be closer to her at the top," Ian said, firmly. "I know it. I can tell."

Drew smiled wistfully into the golden sunshine. "So close, you'll be able to feel her arms around you in a big hug. And she'll be so glad we're remembering her with happiness on this day and not sadness."

A beat of silence passed. "But I am a little sad," Ian admitted.

"I know, pal. That's okay. I am, too."

Ian kicked his toe into the ground as they walked, sending a pinecone skittering. "Do you think she'll like my card? I messed up that one part."

"She'll love it, and it's perfect."

"But, how will it go to heaven?" Ian fretted, shooting another worried glance up at the clouds that were, admittedly, so far away. "I don't get it."

Drew clenched his free hand into a fist. A six-year-old boy's brow shouldn't knit with such worries. At this point, Drew would do or say anything to alleviate his son's distress. If Ian thought the top of the mountain brought them closer to his mommy, then by God, hike they would. He had no plans to dash a little boy's hopeful illusions. "Well, we'll leave it at the top, and when the stars come out, the angels will fly down and carry it up to her."

"For real?"

"Cross my heart."

Ian wore a dubious expression. "But how do you know?"

Think, Drew. Think. He cleared his throat. "Remember that shooting star I showed you last week?"

"Uh-huh. I made a wish."

"Right. Well, that was an angel, coming down to get a message to deliver it to someone else's mommy in heaven."

Ian searched his face for a moment, checking for the truth of his words. Finally he nodded once. "Good." He paused. "But Daddy?"

"Yes?"

"How come there are so many mommies in heaven?"

The question hit Drew like a body slam. "There are a lot of people in heaven, big guy. Not just mommies."

They hiked in relatively calm silence through patches of dappled sunshine for a few moments. When they reached a tunnel of shade created by thick, overarching tree branches, Ian dropped his hand. "I miss her. A lot. Is it okay to say that?"

Drew draped his hand across Ian's shoulders and pulled him closer, fighting the urge to stop, to wrap his arms around Ian, to succumb to the pall of mourning. Neither of them needed that. "Of course. I miss her, too. But let's have a fun day, yeah? The kind your mom would've liked."

"Okay," Ian said. "I don't like being sad."

"Neither do I, Ian. Neither do I."

They managed to get through several minutes talking about the terrain and trees, about the colorful striations in the rocks and what they meant. They managed, just for a little while, to set their grief aside and enjoy a normal father-and-son moment. *Progress*, Drew thought, however small and halting.

A few paces after a switchback carried them once again into the buttery sunlight, they came upon a vast field of stunning, bright-orange flowers—Gina's favorite color. Bright-eyed and happy for the first time in days, Ian stopped short and bounced on the nubby soles of his hiking boots. "Look!" he exclaimed, as if it were a clear sign that his hike-up-high-to-mommy plan had been on-target.

"I see. They're beautiful. Just like Mommy, right?"

"I know. Can I pick some for her? Please? To leave for the star angels so they don't miss my card?"

"Sure, pal. Whatever you'd like." Ian bounded into the field, all cowlicks and energy and thick rubber soles. Drew followed just to the edge. He'd give anything for Ian to be able to give those flowers to his mother in person, but that wasn't possible. As much as losing her had left a gaping hole in their family, Drew was grateful her battle with "the beast," as she'd called it, had ended. That was something, at least. A balm for the soul. Now all he wanted was to see his son happy again, whatever it took.

No more nightmares.

No more depression.

No more bed-wetting.

A boy of his age shouldn't have to deal with those issues. Seeing Ian carefree, running through a field of flowers, Gina's quirky favorite color, brought Drew a modicum of joy he sorely needed, especially on this saddest of days.

Ian whipped back, eyes bright and lively. "Come on!"

"You pick," Drew said, waving him on. "I'll arrange them in a bouquet as you gather them," he said, as if he had the first clue about flower arranging.

Content just to watch his son thoughtfully gather the most beautiful blossoms as a memorial for his mother, Drew sat on a rock jutting out from the edge of the soft blanket of vibrant petals. Honestly? Days like this exhausted him emotionally and physically, straight down to his bones. Gina's birthday, Ian's birthday, Thanksgiving, Christmas, Valentine's Day, his and Gina's wedding anniversary.

Family days.

He'd never planned on being a single father.

And yet, he was determined to do his best, even though a small part of him yearned to curl up and shut out the world until the day was over. Until his pain had eased. Until he could wrap his brain around the logic of a twenty-seven-year-old mother, in this day and age, dying from diabetes. She'd been diagnosed as a teenager, but had never accepted it, a fact that had always pissed him off. The familiar rush of guilt crested inside him, bringing back the times he'd accused Gina of being reckless with her health.

Reckless. He hated that they'd argued about it.

Screaming fights. Tears.

The undeniable truth was, Gina pushed herself too hard, stubbornly determined not to let the diabetes control her life. Instead of managing it, though, she'd laughed in its face. He understood her motivation, but it hadn't worked. It would never work, which is what he'd told her. Why they'd fought. Not that it mattered in the end. Just as he'd feared, the diabetes had won, and he was just the jerk of a husband who'd argued with his headstrong, diabetic wife.

But all that? The past. What mattered now was that he was the grown man while Ian remained a child. Only four years old when Gina died. Drew had shoes older than that. Despite Gina's infuriatingly stubborn nature, she was the mother of his son. Drew simply *had* to keep her alive in Ian's mind, no matter what it took. So? Shutting out the world wasn't an option; his son needed him.

Emotionally flattened, Drew blew out a breath and leaned his hands back on the hot, jagged rock.

The stings ripped through him like little searing shockwaves.

One, then another, and another. And more.

He hadn't even seen the bees.

"Dammit." He flailed, then shot to his feet, spinning this way and that to knock the bees off. How could he have been so careless? Where there are flowers, there are bees. Simple fact of nature.

An immediate rush of heat up his arm set the alarms clanging in his heart. The effects seemed much faster than his usual allergic reactions, which had always been bad enough. But this... probably due to the multiple stings.

Tamping down the panic, he inspected his forearm. Five stings that he could see, already swelling, with hives spreading well beyond the cherry-red bumps. His pulse kicked into overdrive and his face bloomed tight and hot. He recognized the signs of imminent anaphylaxis all too well. He'd been deathly allergic to bees since childhood and had brushed with the life-threatening condition more than once.

This could *not* be happening.

Not today.

He needed to talk to his son before he was no longer able. Needed help. Needed it damn soon. "Ian!" he choked out, coughing through a tightening throat. Damn. His tongue had already begun to swell, as had his windpipe.

Ian pivoted toward him and froze, instantly on alert by the urgency of his dad's tone.

Drew fumbled in his cargo pocket for the EpiPen he never left home without...then stilled. Empty.

No EpiPen? He numbed. Dread spread through him as fast as the bee venom.

He always carried his EpiPen.

Panic pushed through his veins and squeezed him; he couldn't breathe. Shaking, he tore through his other pockets, partially ripping one flap off his hiking shorts. Nothing. He shrugged off his backpack then pawed through it, clumsy and slow, craving oxygen.

Nothing.

Stars burst in his vision as he watched his son run and stumble toward him, the carefully chosen orange wildflowers falling forgotten from the boy's little hand. "Daddy! Daddy! What's wrong?"

He wanted to reassure his son.

Wanted to make it all okay.

But couldn't.

Gasping, choking, Drew sat, then slid back on the rock. He tried to keep the stung arm angled downward, to slow the venom's attack on his body. The skin on his face and hands seemed stretched to its limit, fire-hot and apt to split open if he moved or spoke. When Ian's terrified and confused face appeared above him, Drew didn't have the option of many words. He reminded Ian of the most important ones. "Deer...Track."

He labored for air, his vision blackening. The last thing he heard was Ian yelling for him to wake up.

Eleven-eleven.
Deer Track Trailhead.

Ian repeated the words in his head as he plowed through his daddy's belongings looking for the medicine shot that was supposed to save his life if he ever got stung by a bee. But it wasn't there. It wasn't there! His heart pounded so hard, he could hear it in his head. His throat had gone dry and sore from his heavy breathing.

The shot was *nowhere*.

Daddy had always told him, *use the shot*. But how could he use it if he couldn't find it?

"Mommy!" he wailed in panic and frustration, fists clenched as he glanced up at the fat white cloud.

No answer.

Why couldn't she say something?

Wasn't she supposed to be watching out for them?

He felt so alone. So scared. Tears squeezed out of his eyes. The breeze tilted the orange flowers in the field to one side, then the other. They didn't look so pretty anymore.

Eleven-eleven.

Deer Track Trailhead.

Unsure what to do without the shot, he choked out a sob and shook his dad by the shoulders as hard as he could. It didn't wake him up, but Daddy's cell phone fell out of his shirt pocket just as Ian was about to lapse into full-on hysteria. The cell phone felt like a sign from Mommy.

Help!

He could get help for Daddy. That's what Mommy was trying to tell him. Snatching up the phone, he pressed the three important numbers he'd had memorized since the police officer came to talk to his kindergarten class.

Nine.

One.

One.

Please, God, Ian prayed, as the phone rang. *Don't take my daddy to heaven, too.*

Lexy sat in her glass-walled office overlooking the bustling Troublesome Gulch emergency communications center she managed. The distinctive warble of the incoming 9-1-1 lines carried through the secured room, as did the regular phone sounds, the tones going out to the fire stations and the capable murmurs of the dispatchers she supervised deftly handling calls, emergency and otherwise.

Familiarity.

Her world.

But Lexy's mind wasn't on her work. Her

mood was thoughtful, perhaps even melancholy, which really wasn't her style. But she couldn't seem to shake it and she couldn't figure out why she felt like this. She tossed her pencil aside and studied the three framed wedding photos that adorned the upper left corner of the desk. Her best friends in the world.

Brody and Faith.

Erin and Nate.

Cagney and Jonas.

Survivors from the horrible prom-night tragedy twelve years ago, all of them. Happy. Glowing. Complete. And with their soul mates, at long last, which was all she'd wanted for them since prom night almost thirteen years ago. She'd dedicated her life to helping her friends forgive themselves and move on. That, and to serving her community through her career in emergency services. Both goals served as a sort of…retribution, and only after reaching them could she even think about finding a way to forgive herself for causing the whole thing in the first place—if one existed.

She'd worked in the comm center for eleven years now, and loved it. Giving back to the community kept her sane. And, although it had taken a decade, all her friends had worked through their own pain, come to terms with the past, fully recovered. Brody and Faith had a beautiful baby girl, Mickie, and a teenage foster son, Jason. Erin and Nate had been blessed with little Nate Jr. Cagney and Jonas were still in that newlywed state and probably would be for a while. But they'd more than earned it.

Lexy had done all that she'd set out to do. Mission accomplished.

So…what now?

She'd always imagined she'd feel a sense of serenity, of closure, of having set things right once all the pieces fell into place. But instead she felt restless and afloat, and she had no clue why or what to do about it. Clearly, she'd been so focused on her original goals, she'd never visualized the *what next?* part. Now, here she was, smack in the middle of *what next?* and utterly clueless. Okay, so she'd increased her sessions with the rehabilitation therapist to four times a week—as her sore muscles reminded her—and she felt physically stronger. Emotionally, though, not so much.

She needed something new to strive for.

Like…a hobby? Lame.

A tentative knock on the open door startled Lexy from her contemplative brooding. She shot a glance toward the sound, then exhaled noisily. "Oh, you scared me."

"Sorry." Genean, one of the younger dispatchers, scrunched her nose. "I didn't mean to sneak up."

Lexy easily maneuvered her wheelchair to face her employee, then smiled up at her. "No problem. I was just daydreaming, which, admittedly, isn't listed anywhere in my job description," she added, in a just-between-us-girls tone.

Genean laughed. "Happens to the best of us."

"True enough." Lexy rested her hands in her lap. "What can I do for you, Genean?"

The trendy young woman aimed a thumb toward the central area of the secured room. "Can you sit the board for me for half an hour? I forgot my lunch on the kitchen counter this morning, and I'm sure it's been devoured by my ill-behaved dog by this point." She shrugged. "I've been trying to hold out until I got off shift, but my tummy's protesting loudly."

"Of course." Lexy glanced at the large, wall-mounted LED clock and saw it was already after eleven. Genean's shift had started at six-thirty in the morning. "God, you must be famished. Why didn't you call me down earlier?"

"I was okay until a few minutes ago."

"If you say so. I'd be chewing on paper now if I were you." Lexy winced as she opened her desk drawer and extracted a headset.

"You okay?"

"Just sore. My rehab therapist, Kimberly, has been increasing the intensity of my workouts in preparation for race season." And possibly some experimental therapies, but she didn't share that.

"Physical therapists, personal trainers, they're all evil, if you ask me," Genean said, with a grimace.

"True enough. Kim's a brute." Lexy slipped on her headset, adjusting the earpiece and clipping the cord to her V-neck top. "Give me a quick pass-down of what's going on out there. Then feel free to take your time and have a nice meal. I need the distraction of working the phones today." She gestured toward the door.

Genean preceded her out. "Thanks. As for pass-down, not much to say. Nothing's going on," she said, over her shoulder. "A couple minor medicals, one fender bender with no injuries. But those calls are handled, and the phones are quiet. It's one of those excruciatingly slow days."

Lexy followed her employee down the wide ramp from her office into the center. "G, you know we never utter the phrase 'slow day' out loud," she chided, in a playful tone, as they entered the epicenter of dispatch. "It's the quintessential jinx."

"Oops." Nonplussed, Genean shouldered her handbag and chuckled as she untangled the headset of her iPod from an outside pocket. "Sorry about that."

"G always jinxes us," said Dane, the other dispatcher on duty, currently working the radio side, head buried in the *Rocky Mountain News*. He was senior to Genean, but the two of them got along great and worked well as a team. "She's a crap magnet. Trust me, I know, because I get stuck with her all the dang time," he fake-groused.

"Ha-ha. So not true, Dane. You know you love working with me." She made a face at his back.

"Keep telling yourself that, jinx." He grinned at Lexy, a mischievous gleam in his eyes. "Boss, I've been meaning to ask you about a schedule change."

Lexy shook her head, smiling at their banter.

Genean spread her arms wide. "You people are too superstitious. What could possibly happen in the half hour or so that I'll be gone?"

"Jinx number two, and the worst kind." Lexy

groaned, then pointed toward the exit door. "Go on, get out of here before you lay a hex on the entire town."

"Fine, fine, I know when I'm not wanted." Genean batted her eyes with innocence. "Can I bring either of you anything from the Pinecone?"

"I'll pass," Dane said, burying himself in the paper again. "You'll probably jinx that, too."

Lexy snickered as she plugged into the console and adjusted the height of the motorized ergonomic desktop to accommodate the armrests of her wheelchair. She always loved how dispatch seemed like a family, with "siblings" picking on each other good-naturedly. "Nothing for me, either. I brought lunch. But thanks."

Dane glanced up at his span of five computer monitors, fingers poised over one of four keyboards he manned, as a medic unit called out en route to High Country Medical Center with one patient, nonemergent, followed by additional units going in service, in quarters, or other radio traffic.

Genean gave a little finger wave and left. While Dane was busy communicating with the units on calls, Lexy's restlessness returned like a persistent rash. At odds, she reached into the side pocket of her chair for the sheath of paperwork her care team, led by Dr. Shannon Avolese, had urged her to read.

Experimental treatment.

The possibility of truly walking again, after all this time? Surely she'd never walk without the aid of crutches or, best-case scenario, a cane, but she didn't mind that. For that matter, she didn't mind her chair. It didn't hold her back; she was independent.

Still…walking at all was such a long shot. As it was, the short distances she could walk with crutches exhausted her. But she'd been feeling stronger than ever, physically and mentally. This could occupy her mind for the time being. It wouldn't hurt to try, since she had no emotional attachment to the outcome. It beat collecting stamps, she supposed.

Aside from the initial three years post-injury when rehabilitation had been an everyday thing, she'd resisted the notion of regaining further use of her legs. But experimental treatment options had changed so much recently. She decided to give the literature a once-over, even if she hadn't made up her mind about pursuing it.

Truth was, ever since the prom-night accident, she'd embraced her physical changes as a constant, stark reminder of all the pain she'd caused. She never wanted to forget. Brody and the others suffered from garden variety survivor's guilt, but none of them had truly been at fault for what had happened that night.

None of them, that is, except her.

Lexy shivered, rubbed her palms over her upper arms.

To this day, she could close her eyes and recall the exact moment when she'd irresponsibly tried to crawl on her boyfriend Randy's lap, even knowing he was driving.

Knowing the twisting roads were treacherous at night.

Knowing all of them had been drinking.

She'd known better and had done it anyway.

Her hip hit the steering wheel, knocking it out of Randy's grasp, and the slow-motion look of raw fear on his face before they tipped over the cliff side still haunted her. She saw it as she drifted off to sleep, revisited it in her nightmares and she came back to it as she woke up.

Every day.

He had known he'd lost control of the SUV and, though he tried, there was no regaining it. At that moment, seeing his whitened face, their terrified gazes locked, she'd known, too. It was the last expression she'd ever see him make.

Her fault. No one else's.

If only she could take it all back.

But she couldn't. Four teens buried. It was done.

All things considered, adapting to the loss of function in her legs seemed a small price to pay for the ripple effect of grief she'd set into motion throughout the community.

Still…when she'd confided in Rayna, a fellow wheelchair triathlete, she had suggested that maybe it was time for Lexy to stop punishing herself.

I just don't know how.

She blinked down at the paperwork outlining new treatments. Everyone around her was happy. She supposed she could think about finding a new level of happiness herself, whatever that took. She wasn't sure, though, if this experimental treatment route was the key. If *walking* was the key. It would take her completely out of her comfort zone, and nothing was guaranteed, anyway.

A 9-1-1 line warbled, cutting through the silence. Lexy gratefully tossed the papers aside and pressed the red button on her phone keyboard to engage the line, relieved by the interruption. She'd reconsider the monumental decision about helping herself later. Right now her job was to help someone else, which fell directly *within* her comfort zone.

Go time.

Chapter Two

Calm. Cool. Professional. "Nine-one-one, what is the address of your emergency?"

"Help!" raged a small child on the other end, his screams cutting into the calm of the day. "P-please help me! My daddy's dying."

Lexy's body lurched into full adrenaline alert mode, but she maintained her controlled tone through pure force of habit and years of training. Calls from kids were both the worst and the best. No doubt these crises reached out and grabbed you by the throat, but in her experience, children under stress followed instructions much better than adults. "Okay. Where are you?"

"I…I…"

He sounded young. What if he didn't know his address? She glanced at the ANI-ALI screen, wishing it read differently. But the call had come from a cell phone—no exact location, just the nearest cell tower hit. Dammit. Murphy's Law. "Take a deep breath, honey. I need to know where you are."

"Um…um… D-deers make tracks."

She blinked. "What?"

It came in a breathless tumble of words. "Deer Track T-trailhead. Eleven-eleven. He always has a medicine shot with him but I can't find it."

Medicine shot. High-country trail. Experience told her they were dealing with an allergic reaction. She quickly keyed the unfamiliar trailhead into her computer, then snapped her fingers to get Dane's attention.

He spun around in his chair. Flagging him closer, she pointed at the address field on her computer screen.

Dane leaned forward to read the data, then nodded once and snatched the open-space map out of its upright holder and began flipping pages, tracing the myriad of high-country hiking trails with his index finger.

"Tell me exactly what happened," Lexy said to the caller as Dane tracked down the trailhead.

"I don't know! I w-was pickin' flowers! I think he got stung by a bunch of bees," the boy said, voice wavering and watery. "He's all red and puffy and I can't find the medicine shot thing. I looked everywhere!"

Lexy took a deep breath to keep her own emotions in check. Anaphylactic shock could kill in a matter of ten minutes. And they didn't even have an exact location yet. *Press on.*

"What's your name, hon?"

"Ian," he wailed, sucking in breaths between sobs. "Please, m-my mommy died two years ago today. Please don't let my daddy die, too."

Kick to the gut. Lexy squeezed her eyes shut; her stomach churned with empathy. "Listen to me carefully, Ian," she said almost forcefully before softening her tone. "My name is Lexy and I'm not going to leave you, okay? I'm going to help you through this."

"'K-'kay," Ian said, clinging to her promise like a lifeline. "I'm scared, L-Lexy."

"Be brave for your daddy, Ian, okay? I'm sending paramedics to help him. You can help now by staying calm and answering some important questions. Will you try that?"

"'Kay."

"Good boy. Is your daddy conscious?"

"Huh?"

"Is he awake?"

"N-no, and I don't think he's breathin' very good. He sounds…funny."

Lexy's alert spiked into the red zone. Funny how? she wondered. Funny like the allergic reaction she'd assumed, or funny like agonal breathing just before death? It could be a heart attack, for all she knew. "Do you see bee stings on your daddy? Red bumps?"

"Um…yeah. On his arm. L-lots of 'em."

She keyed that into the notes and hit Save. "Okay. You said eleven-eleven. What's eleven-eleven?"

"We, um…um…started hikin' the Deer Track Trailhead at eleven-eleven. We always m-make our watches m-match just in case something bad happens. Daddy's SUV is parked by the brown sign. Are they comin'? Hurry!"

"We're getting them started. Hang tight."

"Got it," Dane said, in a lowered rasp, tapping his finger once on the map before lunging for his keyboard. Within seconds he'd keyed the exact location into the CAD computer system, set off the pre-alerts and aired the call to the closest units.

Thank God. Lexy flicked a quick glance at the call timer. Ian and his father had been hiking approximately ten minutes when the call came in. They'd be close to the trailhead, but who knew how long the father had been down. "What color is your SUV, Ian?"

"Blue. It's a H-Honda."

"And what's your daddy's name?"

"Drew K-Kimball."

"Okay, good." In her peripheral vision Lexy saw Dane standing to her left, slightly behind her. He was intently listening to her side of the conversation for important details. She pointed to the line she'd just typed in: BLUE HONDA SUV, DREW KIMBALL, signaling for Dane to run a check for the vehicle. She covered the headset microphone with her thumb and told him, "Check under *Andrew,* too."

"Got it," Dane said.

She refocused on her caller. "Stay with me, honey," she said, sounding much calmer than she felt. "You're doing an excellent job."

"'K-'kay. Are they comin', Lexy?"

"Yes, honey, they're on the way. Look around you and tell me exactly what you see on the trail so the paramedics can find you quickly."

"Um…um… Orange f-flowers. A whole gigungus field. We stopped to pick them for the angels to take up to Mommy at the top of the mountain, because orange was her f-f-favorite color." He sucked back a sob and his pitch rose. "Right around a curve after a tree tunnel."

"Okay. Orange flowers. Got it." Despite the continued stabs to her heart with this child's every word, Lexy swallowed back her instinctively human, sympathetic reaction. Sadly, she didn't have time to feel sorrow for Ian, not while his father still needed life-saving help.

She click-clacked the location details into CAD and pushed a button that would transmit it straight to Dane's computer, so he'd have everything he'd need to update the responding units over the radio. They had maybe ten minutes before Ian could quite possibly lose his father.

Could they get there in time?

No clue.

That part was out of her hands. But she needed to engage Ian in the rescue effort, so that regardless of what happened, he'd know he'd done everything he could to help his father. *No regrets.*

A thought struck her. "Ian, do you think the medicine shot is back in your daddy's SUV?" A stretch, she knew.

"I don't know!" came another agonizing wail.

"Ian, honey, take a deep breath for me." She paused, listened to him drag in air and blow it out noisily. "Good boy. Do you have your daddy's keys?"

She heard him fumbling.

"Um…um…yeah! I got 'em from his pocket."

"Good. How fast can you run back to the SUV?"

"I d-don't know. I'm a-scared, Lexy!" he wailed. The wobble in his voice had returned full force. "When are they comin'?"

"Honey, you're being very brave. I know it seems like a long time, but they're coming as fast as possible. Take a breath."

He hiccupped in some air and blew it out.

"Good. Now, listen to me. This is your most important job. I want you to run as fast as you've ever run before and look for that medicine shot, okay? I'll stay on the phone, but if we get disconnected, don't panic. I'll call you right back as soon as we have a signal."

"'K-'kay—"

"Ian, wait. Are you listening?"

"Y-yeah?"

"When you have that shot, you run right back to your daddy fast, fast, fast. Okay?"

"'Kay."

"I'm not going to talk while you run because I don't want to slow you down, but I'll be here if you need me."

"'Kay."

She listened to Ian, footsteps pounding, sucking wind, as he ran back to retrieve the EpiPen she prayed was in the vehicle. Every once in a while, Ian would gasp, "Lexy?"

"I'm here."

"Don't leave me."

"I won't."

Astonishingly, they never lost the signal. Finally, after what seemed an eternity, he said, "I'm here!"

Lexy exhaled, squeezing the bridge of her nose with her fingers. "Check the car, Ian. Take a breath and look carefully."

She heard the unlocking, the scrambling, Ian muttering to himself. A moment passed. "I have it! It fell out on the floor by the um… um…gas pedal."

Lexy crossed her fingers. "Run, Ian. Run back to your daddy and I'll help you give him that shot."

"I…I know how," he gasped out. More pounding. Voice jostling with his steps. "Daddy taught me 'cuz he and I are a team now."

Oh, God. "Good. Run fast."

Adrenaline pumping, she tapped a pen rapidly on the console, her gaze ping-ponging from the call timer to the GPS map on a separate computer that showed the paramedics' progress toward the scene, and back again. She focused on her young caller's panting breaths, counting them.

In, out. In, out. In, out.

One, two. Three, four. Five, six.

"L-Lexy?"

"I'm here, honey."

"Don't leave me."

"I won't leave you."

Finally a shaky-voiced Ian said, "I'm b-back. He's still not awake. He slid off the rock, Lexy. He's on the ground." The panic reared up, making his words higher pitched, thready.

"That's okay. Ian, you can still help him." She had to tamp down his hysteria in order for him to be effective. She flicked a glance at the call timer: seven minutes. Lexy gulped and said a quick prayer in her mind. "Listen to me carefully. Open the package and get the shot ready. Did your daddy teach you that part?"

"Yes. I c-can do it."

"Perfect. Set the phone down and do it. Then pick it back up and tell me when you're done."

"'Kay."

The phone clattered to the ground. She listened to the package being torn, to Ian's heavy breathing, to her own blood surging a staccato rhythm in her ears.

More shuffling. "I'm ready. Lexy?" Ian asked.

"I'm here. I need you to be brave, Ian, because, when I tell you to, you're going to press that needle down into your daddy's leg and hold it there for ten full seconds so he gets all the medicine. That's very important. We'll count the time together, okay?"

"'Kay," he said, in a whimper.

"Now, do as I say. Put the tip of the shot against his upper leg and I'll count to three. Then you'll press down as hard as you can. And we'll count out the seconds."

"W-will it hurt 'im?"

"No, sweetie, not at all. It just may save his life. Be strong for your daddy now, okay?"

"'Kay."

"Ready?"

"Yeah."

"One, two, three—go, Ian."

"I did it!"

"Hold it down hard, no matter what, and let's count," she said in a rush. "One. Two. Three. Four. Five. Six. Seven. Eight. Nine. Ten," they said together.

Nothing.

Lexy held her breath. Dane stood frozen.

Even Ian remained silent.

A muffled, unintelligible groan carried over the line, and Lexy had to blink back tears of relief and clamp her knuckles over her lips to maintain her cool.

"He's wakin' up, Lexy! He's wakin' up!"

She swallowed several times, leveled her tone. "Good, Ian. You did an excellent, excellent job."

"Daddy? Daddy! Wake up!"

"The paramedics are almost there, okay, Ian? And they'll take over. They'll take good care of your daddy."

"Ian?" she heard a deep male voice slur.

As expected, at the sound of his daddy's voice, Ian lapsed into full-blown "refreak," bursting into gut-wrenching, breath-stealing, choking and gagging sobs.

"Ian, hand the phone to your daddy," she said

in a loud, firm tone, before she lost him completely. "Ian!"

Some fumbling, then, "Hello?"

"Drew Kimball?"

"Ah…yeah?"

"My name's Lexy. This is Troublesome Gulch 9-1-1."

"Allergic," he slurred. "Bees."

"I know. Ian told me. Don't try to talk." She could still hear Ian's gulping wails in the background and they tore at her heart. "Just relax right where you are. The epinephrine your son administered will hold you over. Paramedics are almost there to help you, so hang tight."

He blew out a breath. "Yeah. 'S okay, pal. C'mere." A pause. "My son okay?" he asked Lexy.

She smiled for the first time since that line had rung. "Mr. Kimball, Ian is much more than okay. He just saved your life."

Lexy stayed on the line until Drew slurred that the paramedics were tromping up the path toward them, then wished him luck and hit the F8 key to disconnect.

"Holy—" She eased out a long breath and pushed her fingers into her hair, yearning for some kind of an adrenaline dump. "Great job finding that trailhead so fast, Dane."

"Thanks. You, too, boss," he said, admiration threaded through his tone. He wiped perspiration from his temples with the backs of his wrists. "Great job with everything. I heard his wail through your headset when you picked up."

"He was pretty panicked."

"Well, it was one amazing save."

"I'll say" came an unexpected voice from the back of the room.

Lexy swiveled around to find three uniformed men standing at the divider wall, observing the action. Chief Ken Hayward from TG Paramedics had spoken the words. Police Chief Bill Bishop and Fire Chief John Dresden flanked him. All members of the interdepartmental brass had offices one floor above the dispatch center in the main emergency services building, and all of them had radio scanners on their desks. "Chiefs, wow. Sorry, I didn't even hear you guys come in," Lexy said, raising her eyebrows quizzically at Dane.

"Nope, me, neither."

"No worries. We didn't intend to interrupt. Just watching the magic happen," Chief Dresden said. "We headed down as soon as we heard the call go out. You both handled that amazingly well."

"Thank you," Lexy and Dane said together.

Police Chief Bishop stepped forward, gesturing toward the console. "Lexy, how old was that caller?"

"I'm not sure. He was so freaked out, it was hard to get a bead. Young, though. Definitely well under ten. Maybe…five or six? Seven at the most."

"You did a helluva job with him," Chief Bishop said.

Unreal. A compliment like that was huge coming from Chief Bishop, also known to Lexy as her friend Cagney's taskmaster father. But she knew from Cagney that he'd been actively working on changing his ways since his wife left him. Lexy gave him credit for that. She bestowed a genuine smile on him. "Thanks, Chief. Actually, though, the boy's the one who deserves kudos for the save. He did everything I asked of him and more. And get this." She paused. They all waited. "Apparently today is the two-year anniversary of his mother's death."

A murmur of shock rippled through the room.

"Do we know this Drew Kimball?" Chief Dresden asked, eyes narrowed in thought. "Is he local? Name doesn't ring a bell."

"I've met him. He's a recent transplant. Or re-transplant. His family lived here when he was a kid, apparently," Chief Bishop said. "He moved back with his son. Opened that small gym near the youth center, in the old drugstore building."

"Ah, yes."

Lexy had noticed the new gym when she'd dropped by Cagney's. She'd never been inside.

The chiefs exchanged glances. "Once they've got the patient packaged and en route to the hospital, let's get as much information as we can about our young caller," Chief Hayward said. "Sounds like a perfect candidate for the Troublesome Gulch Hero Award, and we haven't had one of those in a while."

Lexy felt her muscles unlocking like a puzzle, her heartbeat returning to normal, pump by pump. "What a great idea. Maybe it'll help to take the edge off this sad day for him. Give him a new memory to associate with it."

Just then, the electronic door beeped, and Genean dance-bopped in carrying white take-out bags and a soda, earbuds from her iPod in and clearly pumping some wildly upbeat tune into her brain. She stopped short, glancing from person to person, then hooked her finger in the white headset cords and yanked the buds from her ears. "Whoa, three chiefs in the room." She widened her eyes at Lexy. "Am I in trouble?"

Lexy shook her head slowly. "No. But I must say, when you jinx the center, Genean, you don't do it halfway."

"Uh-oh. What exactly did I miss?"

Chapter Three

Up on the trail, Drew closed his eyes and felt gradual physical relief seep through him, thanks to the obligatory epinephrine drip and oxygen the paramedics—four of them in all—had administered. Emotionally, though, he was gripped with staggering regret about his carelessness.

Their bonding hike, Ian's card, remembering Gina.

He thought of all the times he'd accused Gina of being reckless with her health, and felt awful. Reckless, careless—it didn't matter which was worse, because they both ultimately impacted Ian.

Drew exhaled sharply, fogging the plastic oxygen mask. He rolled his head to one side on the gurney and saw Ian ask a young, dark-haired paramedic a question, then they both glanced toward him. The paramedic nodded, clapped Ian on the shoulder, then guided him toward the gurney. Ian looked apprehensive, eyes wide. It occurred to Drew that seeing him this way, with tubes in his arms and an oxygen mask obscuring his face, probably reminded Ian of Gina's last day, when the two of them had found her collapsed in the house and had called the paramedics.

Drew struggled to sit up when Ian approached, to remove the mask, to show his son that everything would be okay.

"Try to stay still, Mr. Kimball, while we get you stabilized," said a kindly, gray-haired paramedic with fully tattooed forearms, who seemed to be in charge. "Keep that oxygen mask in place."

Drew raised a palm. "I need to…talk to my son. Please. Just for a moment."

The older man studied him, then nodded. "Try to make it quick."

"Hey, pal," Drew said gently, opening his arms. The younger paramedic lifted Ian to perch on the edge of the gurney, then backed away a few feet.

Ian's body trembled and he wrapped himself as best he could around Drew's middle, his tears starting anew.

"Come on, now, big guy. I'm going to be fine."

The medic shot Drew a sympathetic half smile over the top of Ian's head.

Drew refocused on his son as Ian pulled back, the boy's expression, both watery and hot, challenging him. "Why'd you forget the medicine shot, Daddy? You said we can't be too prepared and then you left it. You *left it!*"

An arrow of guilt, straight to the heart. No excuses. "I know I did. My mind was too full this morning, of your mom, of making sure you and I had a good day. I made a big mistake. I should've been more careful." He paused, pleading with his eyes. "I'm sorry, Ian."

After a moment the boy shrugged one thin shoulder, looking somehow smaller and more vulnerable than he had that morning. "'S okay. But you scared me. A lot."

"I know. But, hey, look how brave you were, even in spite of your fear. You saved my life." Trying for a light tone, he chucked Ian's chin.

"You're a superhero, just like Batman on your backpack."

Ian's lips quivered. "I don't want to be a superhero. I just want you." He glared at the cartoon tough-guy on his discarded pack, an avalanche of emotions crossing through his golden-brown eyes all at once. "Oh, no. Daddy," he said, as if stricken, his tone unsteady, breaths coming quicker. "What about Mommy's card? She won't get it when the angels come down tonight." Panic threaded through his tone. "She's going to think I forgot her."

Dammit. Drew had hoped the subject wouldn't arise. "No. Ian, she won't think that. She's watching us from heaven right now. She knows what happened." Weak argument for a six-year-old who believed he'd be closer to his mom at the top of the peak.

"How do you know?" Ian cried.

"Shh, come here." He held his son closer, smoothing a palm down his back. Somehow, against all odds, he had to make this happen. "We'll…get the card to the top of the mountain, okay? Maybe not today, but—"

"It *has* to be today." Ian's thin chest rose and fell with adamance.

Drew pressed his lips together. Dilemma.

The younger paramedic strode to the one in charge, exchanged a few quick words, then approached him and Ian. "Mr. Kimball? I don't mean to interrupt—"

"It's okay. Name's Drew. Please."

"Drew, then." He pointed to the name tag on his uniform shirt—B. Austin. "I'm Brody. Ian…told me about the hike up to see his mom." His eyes conveyed an understanding Drew hadn't expected. Brody indicated the supervisor with his chin. "Boss here says we're going to chopper you out from the parking lot to get you to High Country Medical Center as quick as possible—"

"Chopper?" Ian shot a wide-eyed glance at Brody.

The paramedic smiled down at him. "You want to fly in a helicopter with your dad, buddy?"

Ian nearly vibrated with excitement, which was a far sight better than his earlier terror and liquid-eyed reproach, if you asked Drew. "Yeah."

"I assume you're going to need your vehicle when you get released, Drew," Brody continued.

"True. Hadn't thought that far ahead."

Brody pressed his lips together. "I know it's not the same for you or Ian—" he shot a quick glance at the boy "—but it just so happens I have something to deliver to the angels for a friend in heaven, too."

Drew understood the paramedic was making this up on the fly, just to assuage Ian's distress. He appreciated the kindness more than he could articulate.

"I'd be happy to carry your mom's card up, too, while you and your dad are in the helicopter. If you'd like."

"Is that okay, Daddy? Will Mommy still get it?"

Drew held the other man's gaze. "You're sure?"

"Absolutely," Brody said. "And it'll serve a dual purpose. I'll keep your keys and drive your SUV down to the hospital so you're not stranded. My rig can pick me up there." He glanced toward the gray-haired man. "Already cleared it with the boss."

Drew rested back on the gurney, suddenly crushed with exhaustion. Or relief. Maybe a combination of the two. After a moment he said, "Ian, go pick some of those flowers, so Mr. Brody can take them with your card. Okay?"

Ian glanced between the two men, then bounded off into the vibrant orange field without a word.

Drew slipped the oxygen mask back in place, grateful for the assistance with his labored breathing. "I don't know what to say. Except thanks," he said, his voice muffled through the plastic. "It's important for him."

"I understand. Really. I'm glad to help out."

"I'm still not used to living in a small town." Drew huffed a wry half laugh. "That's not the kind of paramedic service we'd get in the city."

Brody smiled ruefully. "Oh, trust me. I've worked in big-city departments. That much I know. But Troublesome Gulch is different."

"Yeah. That's why I came back."

"You from the Gulch?"

"Long time ago. I was a kid."

"Ah…missed the small-town grapevine?"

"Something like that." Drew said wearily. In truth, he'd had to get Ian out of the house in Virginia that held so many ghosts. When it came time to decide where to go, Drew could think of no better place to raise his son than the town of all his pleasant childhood memories. It had been easier than he would've imagined to leave his coveted coaching position, pack up their belongings and move west. "We needed a fresh start."

"I know a little something about that." Brody

opened his mouth, then closed it, seeming hesitant to continue. Finally, he crossed his arms. "You know, a lot of us in these parts have experienced losing someone we love. I understand what you're trying to do for your son with the visit to his mom at the top of the hike, and believe me, I know it's not easy. But it's admirable."

"It was Ian's idea. I couldn't dash his dreams."

"I get it. I do." A pause. "Seems like a good kid."

"The best. He keeps me sane."

"He deserves to get that card to his mother." They looked at Ian, carefree for the moment, choosing flowers.

"Yeah." A lump rose to Drew's throat. After a moment, he cleared it away. "You have children, Brody?"

"Sure do." Brody worked his wallet out of his back pocket and extracted a family photograph. He handed it to Drew. "That's Jason, and the baby girl's Mickie."

"A baby and a teenager? That's a houseful."

"Tell me about it," Brody said.

Drew heard the pride in the other man's voice. He pointed to the photo. "And…that's your wife?"

"She's a counselor at the high school. Name's Faith."

"Great photo."

"Thank you."

Drew envied the sound of Brody's seemingly simple, picture-perfect life. He handed the snapshot back, unable to bear talking about it anymore. Not today. "Well, listen. I owe you one. I can't tell you how much I appreciate you doing this."

He watched Brody rub his knuckles against his jaw, hesitating. "Ian says you lost your wife two years ago?"

"Yeah. Seems like just yesterday. She was twenty-seven. Ian was four."

"Helluva thing, man. I'm sorry."

"I am, too."

"What's her name?"

"Gina," Drew said, in a husky tone, appreciating the fact that Brody hadn't used past tense.

Brody nodded, lips pursed. "So, have you met many people since you've been back?"

"Not many. Been…pretty focused on getting Ian settled, opening the gym."

"Figured as much." Brody worked a business card out of his shirt pocket and tucked it in the side pouch of Drew's backpack. "Give me a call sometime when you're feeling better. If you want to. I can introduce Ian to some friends around town."

"He'd like that. Thanks."

"You should join me and some of the other guys for a beer in town sometime. I know my wife would love to watch Ian for an evening. She loves kids."

Drew had to marvel for a moment at the sheer unexpectedness of the offer. It was exactly the kind of small-town warmth he remembered. "I'll do that."

Ian bounded back up, his little hands stuffed full with orange flowers. "Mr. Brody? Here." He thrust over a fistful of blossoms, then peered tentatively at his dad. "Do you like them, Daddy?"

"Love them. You did great, pal. Those are the best flowers in the whole field."

Ian beamed.

"We gotta roll," the gray-haired paramedic said, hiking a thumb over his shoulder in the direction of the parking lot. "Chopper's in the air, and we have cops blocking off the lot to land her. You gonna…"

"Yeah," Brody said, angling his head toward the ascending path.

"Okay, then. See you back there."

Drew watched his son. The prospect of a helicopter ride seemed to have worked wonders on Ian's perspective of the hellish day. Ian stooped and unzipped his Batman backpack, extracting the handmade card and holding it with reverence against his chest. Blinking up at Brody, he said, "Be sure the angels know it's for *my* mommy, okay? Gina Kimball." He studied his card for a moment. "I messed up this part right here, but Daddy says it's still good."

"It's great, buddy. And cross my heart," Brody said, drawing an *X* over his chest with one finger before gently taking the card. He waved it at Ian. "The angels will know exactly who this card is for."

"'Kay."

They started off in separate directions, then Ian stopped short. "Mr. Brody! Wait?"

Brody spun around, then trotted back. "Did I forget something, Ian?"

"Nuh-uh, but do you know a 9-1-1 lady named Lexy?"

Brody grinned. "As a matter of fact, I do. She talks to us and the police officers and firefighters on the radio and sends us out to help people like you and your dad. She's a good friend of mine, too."

Wide-eyed, Ian nodded. "She knows how to save lives, right?" he asked, his tone reverent.

"That she does."

"Will you tell her I said hi?"

"Of course. Run along with your dad and the others, buddy. Get that helicopter ride." He glanced at the precious card. "I'll take good care of this for your mom. Don't you worry."

Ian flung himself around Brody's legs for a quick hug, then trotted back down the path toward Drew, who reached out and took his hand.

More relaxed, Drew settled into the gurney for the ride. The other three paramedics bounced him up the trail toward the parking lot. Unintelligible radio chatter, the clomp of the paramedics' boots, and a rhythmic *whup, whup, whup* of the helicopter rotor overhead cut through the mountain silence. Ian seemed at peace knowing his card would be delivered, and Drew thanked God that a kind voice over the phone had cared enough to help his child through what had to have been a terrifying stretch of minutes alone on the mountain. Fresh guilt stabbed at him.

Strange. In Virginia, he'd never thought of

the people behind 9-1-1 as…well, real people. But this Lexy was a neighbor, a Gulcher. Someone he'd probably run into at the grocery store.

He didn't know the woman. But he owed her.

Big-time.

He closed his eyes and made a mental note to thank her in a day or so for being there for Ian when he couldn't.

For the first time since he'd moved his son away from the home he and Gina had created for their family, Drew felt a sense of rightness about his decision, a tentative thread of belonging, and the fierce desire to rebuild his and Ian's broken lives into something whole again.

Lexy traversed the expanse of polished floor tiles between the bank of elevators and the circular nurses' station. Yvette had been one of the first nurses hired when High Country Medical Center opened after the prom-night tragedy. Lexy could always gauge how busy the day had been by the number of ink pens Yvette had stuck into the ponytail knot on the back of her head.

Three. Hectic day.

Lexy'd have to pull out the kid gloves.

"Hey, Yvette!"

The nurse tucked her chin and peered over her reading glasses. "Well, hello there, Lex. Hang on a sec. Let me type this last note in before I lose my train of thought."

As she listened to the rhythmic clickity-clacking of the keyboard, Lexy glanced at her wristwatch.

Eight-twenty. Darn.

Visiting hours were long over.

She'd planned on being here earlier, but wound up stuck in a meeting about the Trouble-some Gulch Hero Award with the mayor, the chiefs and a couple of council members. But she knew Ian and his dad were on this floor some-where, beyond the iron gates of the nurses' station. If only she could get past the gatekeeper. Brody had texted her earlier to say the doctor had admitted Drew for a night of observation.

She knew it was late, but she wanted to meet the strong little guy from the call, to tell him face-to-face what a great job he'd done. She also asked if she could be the one to surprise him with the news that the city would be honoring him as a hero. It wasn't something that could wait; they wanted to hold the ceremony in a week's time. But she had to convince Yvette to bend the rules.

Which is exactly why Lexy swung by the

diner on her way to the hospital. She glanced down at the bakery box on her lap—the ammo—then back toward the rule-loving nurse in front of her. The blue of the computer screen reflected in the lenses of Yvette's readers as she finished the report.

The older woman hit a couple keys with a flourish, then pulled the glasses off her nose and set them on the counter.

"All done?" Lexy asked.

"All done." She smiled, swiveling her office chair to face Lexy. "So. What brings you to the hospital this evening, young lady? I can probably guess, but—"

"What do you mean? I just wanted to see my very favorite nurse in the world. I've missed you. That's all." Lexy flashed her winningest smile. She knew how rapidly the Troublesome Gulch grapevine worked. Surely the whole town knew about the harrowing 9-1-1 call by now.

"Mmm-hmm." Yvette glanced up at the clock and crossed her arms, but Lexy caught the subtle twitch of her lips. "Why does it sound like somebody has an ulterior motive?" she asked.

Lexy sagged. "Come on, Yvette. I'll only be ten minutes and I'll keep my voice down."

"No can do. The patients need their rest."

"Eight minutes," Lexy implored. "And I'll refill his water while I'm in there and fluff his pillows."

"Already done. Try again."

Lexy held up a bakery box. "Specially ordered peach pie from the Pinecone. Still warm. Eight little minutes."

"It's warm? You fight dirty." Yvette took the box, lifted the lid and inhaled. She narrowed her eyes at Lexy as she mulled it over.

"Please?"

"Fine. *Five* minutes. Room nine. And I'll deny it if you tell anyone I let you break visiting hours."

"You're the best, Vettie," Lexy said. "Enjoy!"

Yvette sighed, reaching into a drawer for a plastic fork. "I swear, the things I'll do for pie."

Lexy wheeled around and headed down the hall. She didn't want to give the woman a chance to change her mind.

The light was low inside the quiet room, but the door stood partially open. She heard the zany *zing-bop!* sounds of the TV playing a cartoon, volume low, and chose not to knock. Instead, she eased the door open wider and entered silently.

A candy-striped curtain drawn halfway blocked her view of the top of the bed, but she could see the snow-white hospital blanket in two peaks near the bottom where it rested over Drew Kimball's feet. The bright cartoon colors kaleidoscoped against the walls of the dim room.

Lexy maneuvered to the foot of the bed, heartbeat steady but fast, anxious to put faces to the voices on the most tense 9-1-1 call she'd handled in a long time.

There they lay, between the metal sidebars of the hospital bed. A big man, curiously innocent-looking in slumber. And, *wow,* gorgeous. Sun-tanned, strong jaw, dark blond hair accented with gold from the sun. And a little boy with similar coloring curled around him, like a koala nestled against the trunk of a tree.

The image snapped her back to her own life, her omnipresent feeling of discontent, and she realized, with a jolt, what was missing. Not a hobby. Not the ability to walk again. She didn't need that to be happy.

She needed…this. The pure love tableau in front of her. She wanted to be the tree trunk to someone's koala. She wanted the kind of un-conditional love a child gave. Why had she never realized—

Lexy stifled a sigh. What good did it do, aching to hear the word *Mommy?* She'd had but one boyfriend, and that had been a high school thing. No boyfriend since, much less a husband, and she wasn't even sure she wanted romance at this point. But, looking at Drew and Ian Kimball, she did feel the unexpected allure of parenthood, out there beyond her grasp.

Ding, ding, went the tones, alerting staff to an emergency announcement. The voice from the hallway speaker crackled through the room's silence. "Dr. Carmody to the Emergency Department, stat. Dr. Carmody, to the Emergency Department, stat."

Drew stirred. Lexy froze.

She desperately wanted not to get caught staring at two sleeping strangers. She rounded toward the door, but heard a familiar little voice.

"Are you another doctor?"

Busted. She turned back, an embarrassed smile on her face. Ian was sitting up in the bed, rubbing his fist into one eye, peering at her with the other. "No, I'm not a doctor." She laid a finger over her lips. "I just wanted to see how your dad is doing, Ian. I'm—"

"Lexy!" Ian exclaimed, his bright eyes widening.

She winced, having forgotten that young kids talked at a high decibel level. "Well, yes, I—"

"I knew it! It's your voice!"

Drew stirred, cleared his throat and woke up. "What's all the racket, pal—" and then he saw her. "Oh. I'm sorry. I didn't know anyone was—"

"Daddy!" Ian cried out, pointing her way. "It's Lexy!"

"Miss Lexy," he reminded her.

"It's Miss Lexy. She talked and I knew it was her. She came to see us!"

Drew's eyes met hers, and Lexy's tummy contracted. "I'm so sorry to have disturbed you, Mr. Kimball. I came by to meet Ian, but I didn't mean for you to wake up." Yvette was going to kill her. "Go on back to sleep. I'll just—"

"No, please. Stay. Ian's been dying to meet you." Drew propped himself on one elbow and fumbled around for the control to raise the upper part of the bed.

Lexy saw it dangling from its cord through the side rails. "Here, let me get that. It fell."

As she moved forward and retrieved the dangling bed-control, Ian scrambled to his knees. "Hey," he said, with the innocent curiosity of a child. "How come you're in that chair, Miss Lexy?"

Chapter Four

Drew blinked when he heard his son's question, and only then noticed Lexy was in a wheelchair. Granted, he'd been pretty much lost in her jungle-green eyes, but still. How could he have missed the chair?

More importantly, how could Ian have *asked* that unbelievably inappropriate question? His stomach plunged with dismay. "Ian. Son, it's rude to ask personal questions when you've just met some—" He watched in frozen horror as Ian, clearly tuning him out at the moment, scrambled over the rails and hurtled himself toward Lexy.

He scaled the side of Lexy's chair and jabbed his way up onto her lap like a little tree monkey with zero forethought about his actions.

Drew cringed inwardly. "Ian! Be careful." His face flamed as he looked into Lexy's almost catlike, tilted eyes. He flipped his hands, sheepish. At a loss for how to make this better. "I'm so…sorry he came at you like a wild animal. I've been trying to break him of that habit, and you can see how well it's going."

To his surprise, Lexy smiled at him, carefree and warm. Instead of handing him the controller, she raised the head of his bed until he sat nearly upright, then lowered the side rail between them. "Is that better?" she asked.

"Uh…yes. Thanks."

She passed him the remote.

He quickly shut off the TV and raked his palm through his hair. "Listen, are you—" *gulp* "—okay?"

"Oh, yes. I'm fine. That's one benefit of paralysis, at least in my case," she said, in an easy tone. "All those bony little knees and elbows don't hurt."

Paralysis.

Drew didn't quite know what to say to that. I'm sorry?

What happened?

It was none of his business, and it didn't matter anyway. He just hadn't pictured Ian's superhero, Lexy, in a wheelchair, he supposed. Then again, he hadn't pictured her at all.

"What's praliss?" Ian asked, gazing reverently into Lexy's eyes. He reached up and twirled some of her dark hair around his finger as if doing so were the most natural thing in the world.

"For Pete's sake, Ian—"

"It's okay. Really. Kids are curious, and I don't mind answering questions." She looked down and chuckled when Ian lifted her locket and examined it, rubbing his fingers along the oval edge. "Frankly, I wish more adults had the courage to just ask me about it instead of tiptoeing around the fact."

"I can understand that," Drew said. He hoped she didn't think he was tiptoeing.

"What is it, Lexy? Praliss."

"Miss Lexy," Drew reminded him of how he'd been taught to politely address an adult.

"What is it, *Miss* Lexy?" Ian asked.

She settled her arm around Ian, and Drew watched him snuggle his head into Lexy's neck the way he used to with Gina. His heart jolted, and he gripped the blanket covering him in his fists.

"Paralysis," she pronounced carefully, "is when you can't move certain parts of your body anymore, honey."

That got his attention. He pulled away to gaze at her. "But you're movin'. I saw you."

"Yes, well. For me, it's my legs. I can move them a little, but not like you or your dad can."

"Why not?"

"I was in a bad car accident a long time ago, when I was a teenager. I injured my spine."

Ian blinked at her, blasé. "So now you can't walk no more? Ever?"

Drew wanted to sink into a hole. He pushed himself into a fully upright position on the bed, then snapped his fingers once to get Ian's attention. "Ian Andrew Kimball," he said, in a low, firm tone, "It's impolite to ask so many nosy questions. Apologize to Miss Lexy."

Ian's happy expression dimmed. "Sorry," he said.

"It's okay, Ian. But you're a good boy for doing what your daddy told you." Her gaze lifted to Drew's face.

She winked, and fireworks exploded inside Drew's body.

"No, I can't walk much anymore. I stand for short bits of time with help, and when I'm feeling really strong, I can move around with two crutches. But it's much easier to use my chair."

"Oh. Does that make you sad?"

Lexy seemed to consider that, as nothing more than a legitimate question from a curious child. "Maybe a little at first, but not anymore. My chair's a tool. I do all the same things I've always done, just a little bit differently. That's all. I used to run, but now I do triathlons using my wheelchair and a special bike. I played on the volleyball team in high school, and I still play, but now it's with other people who use chairs." She waggled her eyebrows at him. "I ski. I dance. I swim almost every day. I even drive my own car. All kinds of fun things."

"That's cool. Can you hike?"

She flicked a quizzical look at Drew. "Hike?"

Drew twisted his mouth to the side. "We hike every weekend. It's our family hobby."

A fleeting shadow moved through Lexy's expression. Or maybe he just imagined it. Either way, her tone was light when she said, "Ah, I see. Well, there are a few hiking trails in Troublesome Gulch that accommodate my chair."

"But not on the regular trails? Not even with those crutches?"

"Ian!" Drew frowned. His face was on fire.

Lexy gave him a look, as if to say, *it's okay.* A beat passed. "Not all of them, no."

"Oh. We love hiking," Ian said, sounding deflated.

"Well, that's good," she said easily. "Hiking is fun." With one arm around Ian's slight shoulders, Lexy held out her hand to Drew. "We're doing this all backward, I'm afraid. I've been so caught up with your son here—"

"As if you had a choice," Drew said, ruefully.

"True." Lexy laughed. "But we haven't formally introduced ourselves. Lexy Cabrera," she said. "Obviously, you're Drew Kimball, of 9-1-1 fame."

"Unfortunate fame, that. But, yes. Yours truly." He slid his palm against her small but surprisingly strong hand.

She sat back. "It's nice to see that you're doing well after this morning's excitement. You gave us quite a scare today. Didn't he, Ian?"

"Yeah. I already told him not to do it ever again. He forgot the medicine shot and he's not s'posed to."

Drew conceded the point with a half shrug,

then adjusted the blanket over his body. He felt vaguely vulnerable in his hospital garb. Uncomfortable. "Yeah. Well, I owe both of you a huge debt of gratitude. You especially, Lexy. Ian told me your voice was the only thing that kept him from being terrified."

"It's true." Ian's serious eyes met hers.

"Aw." Lexy kissed the top of his head. "You kept me from being terrified, too," she said to the boy.

"Nuh-uh, you're not a-scared at all," Ian said, with an air of reverence, his spine straight, tone earnest. "You know how to save lives."

"In case it escaped your attention, he's your number-one fan," Drew said, in an amused tone. "I dearly hope you count a superhero cape as one of your favorite garments."

"No cape." Lexy tossed her hair and smiled, then addressed Ian. "I'm not a superhero, sweetie. I'm just a one-hundred-percent regular woman."

The words caused Drew's abdomen to contract. An air of awareness hung in the room like fog.

One-hundred-percent woman? Definitely.

Regular? No way.

His pulse deepened as an unexpected pull

toward this woman gripped him. Not solely because of the easy, loving manner she had with his son, either, although that was definitely a plus. But aside from that, Lexy Cabrera was, quite frankly, stunning. She wore jeans and a red tank top that showed off tanned and super-toned arms and shoulders. She reminded him of an exotic Marilyn Monroe, all dark, tumbled hair, slanted bedroom eyes and creamy cappuccino skin. Super-sexy without even trying.

Yeah, Lexy was leaps and bounds beyond regular.

But he shouldn't be focusing on that.

"I knew you'd be pretty," Ian told her, as if reading his father's thoughts. "Daddy, isn't Miss Lexy pretty?"

Heat exploded through Drew's body, half embarrassment, half…something else. Because he *had* been looking, and he *had* noticed. And she was…hell, yeah, she was. "I…uh—"

"I tol' him you sounded nice and pretty on the phone, and he said, 'You can't hear pretty, pal,' and I said, 'Yuh-huh, you can, 'cuz I did, and I know Lexy's gonna be pretty.' And see? I was right," Ian declared with triumph.

At least he'd saved Drew from having to answer.

"Well, aren't you the sweetest thing?" Lexy crooned, her face flushing. She pulled Ian into a tight squeeze that made him giggle and squirm, then released him and smoothed down his cowlick. As if it were the most natural thing in the world...

"You look like Jasmine. Doesn't she, Daddy?"

She cast a quizzical look at Drew. "Jasmine?"

Drew opened his mouth to answer, but Ian beat him to it. "You know! The princess from *Aladdin.*"

"She's an, uh, animated cartoon, actually," Drew added, immediately chastising himself in his head. Why in the hell had he said *that?* For God's sake, his six-year-old son had more game than he did. *You'd think I'd never spoken to an attractive woman in my life,* Drew thought with disgust.

"'Cept, Jasmine's just a plain old princess. She's real pretty and stuff, but she doesn't save lives. She does ride on a magic carpet, though."

Lexy laughed, the sound effervescent. "You've raised quite the little charmer, Drew."

"Don't I know it. The kid's smoother than I'll ever be." His gaze tangled with Lexy's for one breathless moment, then she looked away.

"I'll have to look into a magic carpet," she told Ian. "Much cooler than the minivan I drive."

Ian, clearly under the same spell as his father,

blushed crimson and gulped, momentarily shy. "Miss Lexy? Are you somebody's mommy?"

Inwardly, Drew groaned. The boy was the worst kind of wingman. "Geez, Ian. Enough with the interrogation."

Ian scrunched his nose and blinked at him in confusion. "What's that?"

Awkward. What could he say? *It's when you hammer someone with question after godawful question, until your dad's so mortified he wants to disappear?* He cast a pleading look toward their visitor. "At the risk of repeating myself, I'm sorry for the twenty questions." He lifted his arms and let them drop helplessly to the bed. "He's…six."

"Hey, age isn't a factor. Any guy who thinks I look like a Disney princess is okay in my book," she teased. "Looking like a princess is every girl's secret fantasy, you know. That kind of flattery will get him places."

Good to know, Drew thought, before he could stop himself. What was wrong with him? He really *had* gone without oxygen for too long that day.

She tweaked Ian's nose. "No, hon, I'm not anybody's mommy. But I'm the favorite aunt to my best friends' kids."

"They're lucky," Ian said. He let his gaze drift to the floor. "I don't have a mommy no more. She's dead."

Thud.

And there it was. The awkward bomb.

The tone of the conversation completely changed.

For a moment, Drew thought the only sounds in the room were the nearly imperceptible whir of the air-filtration system, the *hum-zap* of the fluorescent lights and the blood pounding in his temples.

Her sobered gaze shot to his face and held, and something about the warm understanding in her eyes made Drew swallow past a suddenly tight throat.

"I'm so sorry to hear that," she said, her words soft and sincere.

He pressed his lips together and nodded. He knew the comment was intended for Ian, but he took a little bit of it into his own heart anyway. "Mommy is your guardian angel, pal. Remember?" he told his son, gently.

"I know." A pause. "But she's not here to tuck me in or play with me," he said.

A strained beat passed. "No, she isn't."

"Daddy? I kinda wish I had an angel mommy

and a real one who can play and bake cookies." He paused, and Drew could see the ideas clicking in his six-year-old brain.

Sirens wailed inside Drew's.

Oh, no.

No!

He could follow Ian's train of thought, but didn't know how to stop him. And if he thought he'd been embarrassed by Ian's nosy questions so far—

"Hey!" Ian's eyes brightened. "Miss Lexy doesn't have no kids. She could be my new mommy."

"Ian," Drew stammered, just as Lexy blushed crimson and said, "Oh," with a whoosh of air. Her hand fluttered up to her locket.

Just then, the nurse with the pens in her hair tapped on the door and raised her eyebrows at Lexy. "Your five minutes were up ten minutes ago, rule-breaker," she said firmly, peering over her reading glasses.

Drew glanced between the two women. Clearly they knew each other.

"Yvette, I was just—"

The nurse crossed her arms and shook her head. "Just nothing. Visiting hours are long gone, and my patient needs his rest."

"Okay, okay." Lexy kissed Ian on the temple. "Jump down, kiddo, before she gives me a shot or something."

He jumped down, but spun to face her. "Miss Lexy, you can't leave!"

Lexy aimed a thumb toward the other woman. "Tell that to Nurse Ratched."

"Ha-ha," the nurse said, with a playful warning scowl toward Lexy. "Your dad needs his rest, little mister," she added, arching her brows at Ian. "And I'm sure it's past your bedtime, too. *Miss Lexy,*" she added, in a pointed tone only the adults caught, "shouldn't be keeping you up so late, and she knows it."

Lexy held up her palms in surrender. "She's right. I'm a horrible influence. I'm going, I'm going. But I'll see you real soon, Ian."

"You will? Where?"

"Yvette—" Lexy waved her in "—come here for one second. I just have to tell Ian and his dad the news I came here to share in the first place, and then I'll skedaddle."

"I'll believe it when I see it." Yvette moved closer and crossed her arms. "So, what's the big news?"

Drew felt Lexy's excitement building. She smiled at his son before aiming those alluring cat eyes his way. "The town has decided to honor Ian as a Troublesome Gulch Hero for saving your life," she said.

Ian began jumping up and down, then bounded up onto the bed. "Daddy! I'm a hero! I'm a hero!"

Drew laughed, in spite of himself, at Ian's unbridled delight. The two ladies joined in. He snuggled Ian close. "You're definitely my hero, pal. That's great," he said, kissing Ian on the cheek before looking toward Lexy. "Wow. So, the hero award. How did this come about? And what does it mean?"

"Well, the police chief suggested it initially. The mayor wants to hold a ceremony in the town square next Saturday, if that works for you," Lexy said. "They asked me to check before the formal announcement goes out."

"Can we, Daddy? Next Saturday?"

"Hmm, I don't know. Don't you have home-work?" Drew teased.

"It's summer!"

"That's right. I think we can mark it on our calendars," Drew said, in a playful tone.

"Tell the police guys yes, Miss Lexy," Ian said.

She laughed. "I will. You'll get a medal from the mayor at the ceremony, plus you get to ride on a fire engine, and your picture will be in the paper. They'll even engrave your name on the hero plaque in city hall."

"And a *cake,* too?" he asked, bouncing his stocking feet on the bed.

The nurse grinned. "Now, there's a kid after my own heart. Plaques, medals and fire trucks are one thing, but give me baked goods any day."

Lexy shook her head and smiled. "I'm sure we can arrange for a cake, Ian. It's not every day we have a real live hero to celebrate, after all."

"Yay!"

A few minutes later, after Lexy and Yvette had said good-night to the Kimball men, they headed toward the nurse's station side by side. Lexy blew out a breath.

"Long day?"

"The longest."

"Stick around for a few minutes and tell me about it," Yvette said. "I'll cut you a piece of that bribe pie."

"You have no idea how good that sounds," Lexy said, with a groan. "Peach pie. And coffee?"

"I've got that, too."

They settled in with their steaming mugs.

Yvette opened the bakery box and took to the pie with a plastic knife. "Whew! What an absolute doll that one is," she mused, lifting the first slice out onto a paper plate and pushing it toward Lexy. She sucked a bit of peach filling from her thumb.

"No kidding." Lexy turned her pie so the crust faced her and forked into the back side. She liked to keep the tip for last. "Give that boy about ten years, and he's going to break teenage hearts left and right."

The plastic knife stilled in Yvette's hand, and she blinked. "Oh, Ian? Sorry, I was talking about the older male in the room. The tall, sexy, muscular one? He takes 'hot daddy' to a new level."

"Yvette!" Lexy shot a glance toward Drew's door and laid a finger across her lips.

"What? They're not going to hear me." She sniffed, finished cutting, then plopped the second wedge onto a plate for herself. "Plus, don't avoid the subject."

"What subject? I didn't even know we were talking about Drew."

Yvette pinned her with a droll stare. "Even you have to admit, he's the most gorgeous new resident to cross the city limits of Troublesome Gulch in a good long time." She leaned in. "And he's single," she stage-whispered, before waggling her eyebrows suggestively.

"He's not *single*. He's widowed."

"Same difference."

Lexy plucked at the seam of her jeans, feeling overheated and itchy. "Whatever. Anyway, I wouldn't know," she fibbed. "I wasn't looking at him. I don't date."

"No?" Yvette raised her eyebrows. "Well, perhaps you should, cupcake. The bloom's not off your rose yet."

Lexy's tummy plunged and fluttered, but she did her best to hide it. She glared at Yvette. "Eat your pie, Nurse Ratched. I'm *not* looking for a date."

"More's the pity," Yvette said, after swallowing her bite of pie. In a fake southern drawl, she added, "If I looked like you, *Miss Lexy,* I'd have a new one every weekend."

"You are pure evil." Lexy stuffed a bite of pie into her mouth and concentrated on chewing. Truthfully? She'd gotten an eyeful of Drew Kimball herself, and yes, the man made her pulse race. But she wasn't sure he had any interest in dating after all she'd heard about his late wife. Clearly, he hadn't moved on.

As if she had?

Her palms went cold at the thought. Okay, so she hadn't dated since Randy, but that had been her choice. After a couple years, she hadn't wanted to. Hadn't even thought about it. It just dried up, that desire. She'd had other, more important things on her mind.

But, what if she wanted to?

You don't deserve it, Lexy.

She shivered, pushed away the omnipresent thought that ribboned through her head. Maybe she didn't feel deserving, but if she did, would she really set her sights on a widower and his young son whose favorite hobby was *hiking,* for God's sake? Couldn't they at least be avid swimmers?

It didn't matter anyway, because once Drew found out about her, about what she'd done, he'd realize just what kind of a person she was and it would be game over. Plus, there was the rest of it. She hadn't been with anyone since the accident....

A cloying awfulness stole her breath. Oh, my God. For the first time in a decade, Lexy was rocked by the realization that she felt self-conscious of her chair, resentful of the very tool that she used to stay mobile, active and independent.

And that simple fact left her awash in shame. Her friends and family loved her; the chair didn't matter to them. It didn't matter to her, either. In fact, quite the opposite—she appreciated it. If the simple idea of dating a man made her worry about her chair? Well, then, she'd rather not bother. She didn't need romance to make her life complete. Didn't deserve a boyfriend *nor* did she need a hobby. And no, she wasn't anyone's superwoman.

She was fine with her life exactly as it was.

Ask anyone.

That traitorous voice inside her whispered, *who exactly are you trying to convince?*

Chapter Five

Deep down, Drew knew something had changed for him.

On the surface, his life appeared normal. Status quo. Business as usual. Same Drew, different day. He'd like to blame his current, inane train of thought on Ian's hero worship and mommy obsession and nonstop chatter about the woman who could "save lives," but a man could only lie to himself for so long.

This was about Lexy, not Ian.

He'd seen her once, right? *Once*. And he hadn't stopped thinking about her since. Drew wracked his brain. Honestly, he hadn't thought of a woman—any woman—since Gina had died, not even when his former colleagues had tried to nudge him back into the deep end of the dating pool six months ago.

You aren't getting any younger, Kimball.

She's hot, and she really wants to meet you.

What could it hurt? Might do you good.

He'd loved Gina, sure, but she'd been a bright, dangerous flame, and he'd wound up burned. He'd always claimed Ian wasn't ready for a new female in his life, but the truth was, no one, not even the so-called "hot ones," had intrigued him enough to pull him out of his comfort zone. No one, that is, until now. But was Lexy even interested?

Drew engaged his blinker, looked both ways, turned left. "Stupid."

"Huh?"

Drew glanced into the rearview mirror; Ian stared up from his little handheld video game. "Nothing, pal. Just thinking out loud."

Ian went back to his game, Drew to his inane thoughts. The thing was, he didn't even know Lexy, not really. Didn't know if she dated, if she even had any interest. Didn't know what dating a woman with her physical differences would entail. He'd be lying if he said that hadn't crossed his mind. Yes, she seemed worth pursuing, and anyone with eyes and a libido could see her beauty. He'd even paid attention earlier that week when Ian had played his *Aladdin* DVD, just to get a glimpse of Princess Jasmine. The "animated cartoon character" Ian thought she resembled.

God. Had Drew really said that to her?

Clearly, he was delusional.

But, the sobering fact was, Lexy had set up camp in his mind since she had visited him and Ian in the hospital, and he wanted to know more. Those slanted green eyes, the easy way she had with his son. Her hair. God, her hair.

He was curious about her, about the way she lived, if she had someone special in her life. He wanted to hear more about her accident, more about her athletic pursuits, more about everything that made Lexy…Lexy.

"Stupid," he muttered.

"Thinkin' out loud again?" Ian asked.

Drew hadn't even realized he'd spoken. "Yeah, I guess so." He claimed *Ian* was starry-eyed about the woman, but then again, everyone always said the boy had his eyes.

"Are we there yet?" Ian asked, with a seriously put-upon sigh.

Drew glanced at the clock on his dashboard. Fifteen minutes until the Troublesome Gulch Hero ceremony kicked off, which set his nerves alight beneath his skin. He tightened his grip on the wheel. "Almost."

"Why's it always take forever to get someplace when you're excited?" Ian groused.

So, so true. His boy was nothing if not astute.

"It's called anticipation."

"Well, I don't like it."

"Me neither, pal." Just like fear, anticipation stretched time until it was nearly unbearable. The boy had been looking forward to this event for a week, but Drew knew it had felt like an eternity. Hell, it had felt like an eternity to Drew, all because of Lexy. Ian wanted his medal and all the hero trimmings, for sure, but he was most excited to see Lexy, too.

Drew smirked. Like son, like father.

And yet, the fact remained. Drew knew nothing of substance about Lexy. He knew nothing about her health, and the thought of getting involved with another woman who had health concerns, who took risks, the thought of putting Ian into

the position of getting his heart broken again—
it was the last thing he'd do.

Regret and fear kicked him. Repeatedly.

Thump, thump. Thump, thump.

It took a moment for Drew to realize it was
actually Ian bouncing the toes of his good shoes
against the back of the driver's seat. "Don't kick
the seat, please."

Ian did as he was told, but tossed out another
melodramatic sigh. "Now are we there?"

"We are."

"We are?" Ian's tone changed. "For real?"

"Yes. Look out the window." Drew paused.
"See all those people?"

"In the park?"

"That's the town square."

"Oh. Looks like a park."

"It's kind of a park," he conceded.

"What's all those people doing?"

"Waiting for the guest of honor."

"The who?"

Drew glanced at his son in the rearview
mirror. "You, goof. You're the hero, remember?
Heroes are always guests of honor."

After a long pause, Ian simply said, "Oh."

Drew crunched into the packed asphalt parking lot and found a spot in the back row. Claim-

ing it, he cut the engine, then released his seat belt and twisted to face his wide-eyed son. "Ian? You okay?"

"All those people are here for me?"

"You bet."

Ian lapsed into stunned silence, pressing his back against the seat. "But we don't know that many people," he said, sounding surprised and a little nervous. Which wasn't like him. He'd always been a sociable boy, at least until he'd lost his mother. Until his father drew him close and kept him sheltered.

Too sheltered, maybe? Too much Dad time? For far too long?

More regrets.

"Do we, Daddy?"

"Hmm?"

"Know those people?"

"We don't know all of them." Drew swallowed through the guilt brought on by his sobering realization and tried for a nonchalant tone. "But Miss Lexy will be here. You know her, right?"

Ian crossed his feet at the ankle, making no move to unbuckle. "Did she bring all those strangers?"

Drew rested his hand on Ian's knee. "They're folks who live in town, Ian. They're here to celebrate with you. Neighbors, not strangers."

"Oh." A pause. A crinkled nose. "Our neighbors?"

Drew cocked his head. This hesitancy wasn't like Ian. "What's wrong, son?"

"I dunno." He chewed on one corner of his lip, ignoring the question. "Who else do we know here?"

"Well, I'm not a hundred percent sure yet." He thought hard. "But I'd bet Nurse Yvette, from the hospital, will come. You liked her, right?"

Ian nodded. "She gave me a piece of pie in the middle of the night when you were sleepin'."

"She did?"

"Yeah. 'Cept I wasn't s'posed to tell you, so don't say anything to get me in trouble."

Drew smiled at him.

Ian rolled an idea around in his head. "And what about Mr. Brody?"

"I'm sure he'll be here, too. And the other paramedics who helped us."

"Oh."

Drew reached back and squeezed one of Ian's shoes. "You'll know a lot of people once we get out there. You might even meet some kids. Make some new friends. And I'll be right with you the whole time. Okay?"

Ian wound his fingers together, his gaze never leaving the grassy square teeming with strangers. "I kinda just wish I could see Miss Lexy."

"I know."

Ian's pointed gaze was too direct, too insightful. "Do you wanna see her, too?"

A beat passed. More than Ian could possibly know. "Sure. I'm looking forward to seeing everyone. And don't forget, we get to have cake." *Nice save, Kimball.*

"My tummy doesn't feel like eatin' anything. It's all tumbly and gross."

"Not now, maybe, but that's just nerves. Your tummy will be fine later. I know how you get around cake."

Undeterred, Ian asked, "Daddy, is Miss Lexy our friend? Like, our real friend?"

"Well," Drew hedged, "we just met her."

"But she helped me. And she visited us. And she's really nice and pretty and saves lives." He twisted his lips to the side. "I want her to be our friend. Really a whole lot."

"So you've said. We'll see what we can do." He couldn't make promises until he checked out the situation. Instead, he bought time getting

out of the SUV and opening Ian's door. "Unbuckle, pal. Let's get going so you can see Miss
Lexy and the others."

Ian did as he was told but made no move to
head toward the throng. "Do we *have* friends
anymore, Daddy? Like we used to in Virginia?"

Drew stood back and let Ian leap out of the
vehicle. "Sure we do," he fibbed.

"Then how come no one ever comes over to
our house?"

Another thud of regret dropped to the pit of
Drew's stomach. He'd been trying so hard to
keep everything together, but obviously he'd let
it all fall apart. He managed to keep his tone
light. "I guess because we haven't invited them."

"How come?"

"Well, we just moved here."

"We've been here forever," Ian said, with a
groan, flapping his arms out to the side and
letting them drop.

"Three months is only forever when you're
six years old." He hesitated. "The house isn't all
fixed up yet, that's all." He still had boxes
stacked in some of the rooms, a fact that embarrassed him.

"How come it isn't?"

Kids. "Because your dad's been busy opening

the gym and answering all your millions of questions, and there's only so much time in the day." He swung Ian up into his arms for a hug that made the boy giggle until he squirmed to be set down. Drew squatted and adjusted Ian's slacks and tucked in the part of his shirt that had come untucked. He had to give his son more than pat answers. "Tell you what. We can start on the rest of the house today when we get home, if you'd like."

Ian slid his hand into his father's and they headed toward the throng. "And when it's all fixed up, we'll invite our friends over? For a big, giant party?"

God, a big party. Drew's jaw clenched. "You bet."

"The friends from Virginia?"

He chuckled softly. "I don't know about that. It's a little far for them to drive."

"Then our new friends instead?"

"Sure."

"We gotta make some, then."

A beat passed. "Okay."

"Starting with Miss Lexy."

Kids, Drew thought again. Like little coyotes. They circled a target, slowly, but they always trapped it in the end. "Okay. We'll see," Drew said. "For now, let's enjoy your hero ceremony, okay?"

"'Kay! But we'll tell everyone they can come to our house for a party as soon as we finally take all our junk out of the packin' boxes and put it away."

Drew laughed. "Let's keep that one to ourselves."

Thankfully, Ian's questions ended as he stared out at the festive crowd. They'd scored a perfect Rocky Mountain day for the ceremony, complete with a cloudless, deep blue sky and a light breeze to keep the blazing sun at bay. In addition to those who milled about, elderly ladies in sun hats perched on the temporary bleachers the city had erected. Families shared bright blankets laid over the grass. Music from two big speakers carried on the breeze, mingling with the fruity fragrance of summer.

Though he'd played it off for Ian's sake, it surprised Drew to see how many strangers had shown up simply to honor one little boy's heroics. *Neighbors, not strangers.* He'd wanted this small-town atmosphere for Ian; it's why he had left a lucrative career he loved to move here. But the coziness still caught him off guard now and then. He needed to loosen up. Maybe Lexy could help him meet people....

And clearly, as Brody had said, the grapevine hummed with what had happened. All week, Gulchers he'd never met had reached out. Stacks of cards and letters for Ian arrived daily at the gym, some with a five-dollar bill tucked in, or a small gift. Warm gestures like these went a long way toward prying open Drew's self-protective shell. They'd moved to Troublesome Gulch for a fresh start, after all. Ian was ready.

Now was the time to grab for it.

A vision of Lexy undulated through his mind; his breathing shallowed. He had to get it together, regain his bearings. He didn't have the luxury of being drawn to a woman he knew nothing about. Just because Ian had perched her high up on a pedestal, just because she *wasn't somebody's mommy?* That didn't mean anything. She could be married. She could be completely uninterested. And, even if she wasn't, who was to say—

"Stupid," he said.

"Da-addy!"

"I'm sorry, pal."

"My kinny-garden teacher always tol' me I was s'posed to think with my head, not with my mouth."

"Smart woman." Drew winked at his son.

But…really. Stupid wasn't an overstatement. He couldn't afford to get swept up in Ian's fantasy. Fact: Lexy had merely stopped by the hospital to meet Ian, to give them the news about the award. Like sending cards and showing up for an award presented to a six-year-old boy, that's what small-town folks did. It didn't *mean* anything.

Did he want it to mean something?

Did he?

He couldn't answer that, not without seeing her again, to get a feel for the situation, for *her* situation. But seeing her in front of the whole town, among people she knew and who knew her? He'd never admit it out loud, but the prospect was a bit daunting.

Ian, on the other hand, had overcome his momentary, uncharacteristic shyness and vibrated with excitement. He yanked on Drew's arm. "Walk faster, Daddy."

"I'm coming, I'm coming." Drew's throat went dry. So many unfamiliar faces.

People he didn't know.

Hadn't taken the time to know.

Hadn't thought he needed to know.

Now he didn't have a choice.

"Daddy?"

"Yes?"

"Lexy could be a mommy if she wanted to, right? Even though she can't walk and stuff?"

Besides the fact that Drew had no clue, they'd dissected this line of thinking repeatedly over the week and it wasn't helping his mind-set. He didn't have the strength to get into it now. It wasn't Ian's fault. The kid missed his mother—who could blame him? But Drew couldn't handle him bringing that up in front of Troublesome Gulch proper.

It's been two years. It's Ian's life, too.

"You know what we talked about, Ian. I don't want you acting nosy around Miss Lexy. Please don't ask her that question. Be polite, okay?"

"I'm just curious. You know, if she wants to. If she likes kids and stuff."

That makes two of us....

The week had been a nightmare, culminating with today.

Lexy had just transferred to her chair and raised the ramp from her van when her cell phone rang. She slammed the door, then punched the button to her headset as she made her way toward the grassy town square. "Hello?"

"Where *are* you?" her friend Faith demanded.

"I'm here, I'm here. I was running late."

"She's running late," Faith said to someone else, in an incredulous tone. Lexy knew this would raise questions for her friends. If she was one thing *always,* it was punctual.

Lexy heard Cagney say, "You're kidding me. Why?"

"No clue, but that's what she said," Faith murmured, then into the phone, she added, "Here, where?"

Lexy rolled her eyes. The thing is, she wouldn't have been late if she hadn't completely freaked herself out about being honored alongside Ian Kimball. She didn't deserve to be called a hero, and she didn't want it. Plus, she'd changed clothes a zillion times, which of course smeared her makeup and jacked up her hair. At the last minute, she'd thrown on her original outfit, repaired her makeup as best she could, fluffed her hair and flown out the door. But she was still pushing it, time-wise, and now her friends were suspicious.

Exactly what she didn't need.

"I'm coming from the parking lot," she said, trying not to sound testy. "How much time do I have before it starts?"

"Barely any. Hang on."

Lexy heard deep, muffled voices through the phone.

"Where in the lot, Lex? Be specific," Faith said. "I sent Brody and Jason up to hunt you down. They said they didn't see your van."

"I don't need to be hunted down. I'm coming. Anyway, I parked in the courthouse lot, sorry. They still haven't fixed that buckled piece of concrete at the edge of the other lot and I'm sick of maneuvering around it. This is the smoothest access into the square." She glanced out over the crowd, and a flock of chickens inside her tummy started to peck and squawk. God, she didn't want to be held up to the community as anyone's standard. Least of all, Ian's. "Meet me up near the podium, okay? I'll be there in a sec."

"Hurry!"

Lexy disconnected and tucked her phone earpiece into the side pocket of her chair. She shoved forward and let the rubber of her handrims skim beneath her palms as she sped dangerously down the courthouse's ramp, toward the wooden pathway that led to the portable dance floor they'd set up instead of a raised platform, in deference to her. At the bottom, she gripped the brakes hard to slow down, then looked around.

People soaked up the warm sunshine, chatting and laughing, totally oblivious to her inner turmoil. She may have cut it close, but she'd made it in time.

Breathing deeply to calm her frazzled nerves, Lexy scanned the crowd for Ian. *Inhale.* And, okay, Drew. *Exhale.* Definitely Drew. "Stupid," she muttered. The man knew nothing about the real her. The imperfect, unworthy, tormented Lexy Cabrera.

She pressed a palm to her abdomen to quell her anxiety about seeing him again. Anxiety? Or was it poorly thought-out anticipation? Whichever, she didn't see them. Pushing forward, she came around the back side of the podium and skidded to a stop behind her best friends: Cagney and Jonas, Erin and Nate and Faith.

"Where's Brody?"

The group turned to face her.

"Whoa," Erin said, her eyes going round.

Dead silence.

"What?" Lexy looked from one friend to the other. No one said anything. "*What?* Hello? Will someone please translate? I don't speak monosyllabic pseudo-grunts under a time crunch, sorry."

With a smirk, Jonas said, "I think she meant, whoa, look at Lexy bringing sexy back, in a world-class way." He whistled low, then stepped back to sweep her with an appreciative glance. "You look…wow."

"Oh, please." Lexy played it off with a scoff. "It's just a sundress. I'm *so* not—"

"You so *are*," Faith said, with a gleam in her eye. "And you so know it." She crossed her arms and bounced on her heels. "Do tell, Lex, who's the extra effort and brand-new dress for? I mean, we're impressed, obviously, but we're always impressed by you."

"It's not new, it's new*ish*." Lie. It was new. "And it's not *for* anyone," Lexy said, peevishly, trying to ignore the hot flush moving up her neck. Okay, so maybe the dark fuchsia halter dress tipped the sexy scales a *little*, but it was still professional. But the sexy factor wasn't why she'd bought it. It was flowy and knee-skimming, and it looked good against her olive skin tone. If the deep V and empire waist *happened* to enhance her cleavage in a big way, okay. Bonus. But, that wasn't exactly her fault. Nor was she to blame for the way her locket…nestled just so within that V.

It's not as if she made the damn jewelry.

She'd just needed to feel...better about herself today, because she'd felt nothing but bad and progressively worse since visiting the Kimball men in the hospital.

"Need I remind you, I'm representing the comm center? I have to be in front of the whole town. I'm just trying for a professional yet festive look."

"You mean the whole town, who's known you since you were a baby and doesn't care how you look?" Cagney asked, in that thoughtful, observant way of hers.

Point taken. "So? What—you want me to wear sweats to a hero presentation? I have to look nice."

"There's looking nice," Nate said, with a playful narrowing of his eyes, "and then there's being so hot you render you friends mute." He lifted her hand and twirled her chair around in a circle. "Lexy, seriously."

She forced a smile, heat creeping up her face. "Thanks, Nate. You're a gracious man. Everybody, you're all sweet, really. But I didn't take any more effort today than I do on any normal day." *Big, honking lie.* She didn't feel worthy of this award, or of the crush she seemed to have on Drew Kimball, but she'd damn well try to look worthy, if nothing else.

"Right." Erin pursed her lips in scrutiny. "Is that a new lipstick color, too?"

Lexy groaned. "Geez, is Big Brother watching?"

"Answer. Is it new?" Faith reiterated.

"Look, I was at the salon the other day and I grabbed a tube. Whatever. It matched the dress. It doesn't mean anything when a woman buys a new lipstick." Her chair wobbled slightly. She shot a glance at Faith, whose hand was currently stuffed into the little ditty bag that snapped onto the arm rest. "Hey, what are you—?"

"Aha!" Faith held up the shiny black lipstick tube as if she'd found a smoking gun. She squinted at the tiny label on the end. "Interestingly enough, ladies and gents, the shade's called *Manhunting.*"

"Don't be ridiculous," Lexy said, in as arch a tone as she could muster, what with being thrown so totally off-kilter by the rapid-fire interrogation. Her friends were looking for clues to a mystery that didn't exist, and suddenly she verged on tears. "Did I name the thing?"

"Come on. You can tell us. Is it Dane from work?" Erin asked, in a conspiratorial whisper. Her eyes danced with curiosity. "I've always thought he was a cutie."

Lexy squeaked a protest. "Are you high? He's

a twenty-five-year-old who also works for me. Geez, what kind of a morally devoid lech do you think I am?" She scissored her hands in front of her. "Seriously, lay off, guys. I have to be on-stage soon, and you're stressing me out more than I'm already stressed out."

"Fine, fine," Faith said, as she replaced the lipstick in the little bag. "But we'll get the goods out of you sooner or later."

"There's nothing to *get*," Lexy said, but she knew she was blushing.

"Lex?" The ever-observant Cagney asked, her blond head tilted curiously to the side. "Is everything okay, hon?"

To her horror, Lexy's chin quivered once, and she opened her mouth to speak—

"Hey, Lex," Brody called out through a cupped hand, from a few feet away. *Saved by the yell.* Then again, maybe not. Two men and a boy loped toward them, all smiles. "Look who I ran into."

"Miss Lexy!" she heard, just before Ian bar-reled toward her and hurled himself into her lap.

"Oof!" she said, laughing. Which was better than crying any day. The moment he'd settled in her lap, she felt more relaxed. Focused. Serene. "Hey, honeybunch. How's my little hero?"

"Ian Kimball," Drew said, rushing forward with concern clouding his eyes. He squatted before her chair, bringing him eye-to-eye with his son. "How many times do I have to tell you not to plow into people?"

"Sorry," Ian said to Lexy, by rote, before turning back to his father. "But it's Miss Lexy, Daddy. I haven't seen her in a really, really, really long time." He curled, unabashed, into the curve of her shoulder.

Drew shook his head, then smiled into her eyes. "At the risk of repeating myself, I apologize for the little monkey's bad manners."

"No worries."

She swallowed, albeit with a bit of difficulty. God, she wouldn't have believed it possible, but he was a thousand times hotter out of bed than in it.

A hospital bed, that is.

In jeans and a loose-fitting, cream-colored shirt that skimmed his shoulder muscles and hinted at taut abs, Drew Kimball was the person bringing sexy back, not her. And he would never be hers. Not in a million years. This was bad, bad, bad news. "It's—" *gulp* "—good to see you again," she said, trying not to let her inexplicable feelings come through in those six little words. Failed miserably, of course.

He wouldn't catch it, but her nosy friends would.

"A-and, you look good," she added, quickly. "Much better, I mean."

"You, too. You look…wow, really great."

"Hello?" Faith prompted, spreading her arms wide.

"Oh, sorry." Lexy didn't have to look at her friends to know what they were assuming. They had, after all, disappeared to her the moment she'd seen Drew, like the Tony and Maria dance scene from *West Side Story*. She could almost hear their brains ticking, and felt like a puzzle they were frantically piecing together. Little did they know, the puzzle was missing that warm, beating red piece directly in the center.

Bracing herself, she waved a wan hand toward the crowd. "Everyone? Drew and Ian Kimball. Drew, these are my borderline-annoying friends. I can't be held responsible for anything they may blurt out. It's a full pack, so I'll leave the introductions to them."

As everyone took their time sharing hand-shakes, hugs and names, Lexy slumped in her chair, enjoying the simple warmth of Ian against her shoulder, but feeling trapped and scared. Not by this sweet little boy, but by the imminent, inevitable questions her friends would pummel her with. Questions for which she had no answers.

True, she was the only one in their group who hadn't gotten married. But, ever since Cagney and Jonas had reunited, everyone seemed to be hell-bent on a mission to remedy that. They didn't understand….

She just prayed they wouldn't say anything mortifying in front of Drew or Ian. It was bad enough that they'd draw conclusions and demand details when none existed.

But, ridiculously, after all she'd told herself she didn't need—nor did she want romance, a man, love—she still *wished* such details existed with her and Drew.

That's the thing.

She wished she was worthy of a man like Drew Kimball. She couldn't deny an inexplicable pull toward him and his adorable, energetic son. Being around them soothed the restlessness inside her, but it was a dead end, and she knew it. Just her luck, being attracted to a man who seemed to be still mourning his late wife. A man whose hobby she'd never share. A man who wasn't looking.

A man. *Sigh.*

Face it, Lex, you're scared.

A shudder ran through her. Sure, she was scared. Or maybe just realistic. Drew and Ian and all of Troublesome Gulch had built her up to be some kind of a superwoman. Her friends had her pegged as some sort of a catch. Frankly, she wasn't either one. Just the opposite. The more she thought about it, the more panicky she felt. Once Drew and Ian knew the truth about her…

Couple that with the fact that she knew any man who'd even want to fall for her, with all her differences, would have to be someone special. Not that Drew wasn't, but she didn't know and didn't feel ready to put herself out there, to risk that kind of possible pain. Moot point. She still felt so wholeheartedly undeserving of unconditional love.

Wimp.

The thing was, she and Drew could be friends, right? Friends worked. The whole friendship thing was all she'd allowed herself for years.

So this time why did friendship feel like… not enough?

"Stupid," she muttered.

Ian whipped a glance at her. "Hey, that's what Daddy kept saying on the way here." He scrambled off her lap and bounced toward his father.

Her gaze shot to Drew's and held for a second. Was it her imagination, or did he look as alarmed as she felt?

Faith leaned toward her ear as the men engaged Drew, and eventually Ian, in conversation. "The lipstick name makes all the sense in the world now," she whispered, in a smug drawl. "He is hot."

"Please stop," Lexy said, her voice shaky. "It's just a coincidence. I'm not interested in him. I'm not interested in anyone. And I don't want to be forced in that direction."

"Why not?"

A pause. "Just don't say a word, Faith, I'm serious."

Faith smirked as if she knew a secret, but what she didn't realize was that Lexy wanted to bolt. She wanted the safety of her world, her job, her solitude. She didn't want these issues of worth and guilt, need and yearning, cropping up in her life again.

Perfect match to the dress or not, Lexy vehemently regretted that lipstick purchase. The last thing she needed was a pack of matchmakers breathing down her neck when, depressingly, there wasn't a match to be made. Not that she had a choice in the matter, knowing her friends.

She eased out a breath of tension.

Let the games begin.

Chapter Six

It wouldn't go away.

Dammit. What was it about Drew Kimball?

That's what she couldn't figure out.

He was just a man, right? Like every other man. She worked with men, she had male friends. Men walked through her world on a regular basis. So why did *this* man make her do something crazy like buy a new dress, for God's sake, and matching lipstick to boot? When he'd never expressed so much as one iota of interest in her? When she'd so much as told herself she wasn't anywhere near ready to risk it?

Lexy tapped her fingertips against her lips and studied him through dark sunglasses that masked the direction of her gaze. All her friends had, thankfully, laid off the twenty questions after growing bored with her nonanswers. They'd wandered off in various directions to enjoy the post-ceremony socializing. She was finally free to observe without being observed, to brood. She needed the time to figure out the riddle that was Drew Kimball.

Phew, did she ever.

One benefit her chair provided was a semblance of invisibility whenever she wanted it. She'd never struggled to be noticed, and the accident hadn't changed that. The chair hadn't stood in her way of being seen as *Lexy,* because she hadn't allowed that. But when she *wanted* to retreat, like now, it came in super-handy.

She eased her way slightly out of the fray, adjacent to the refreshments table, and settled in to…people-watch.

You can lie to the world, but don't lie to yourself.

Okay. Drew-watch.

It had to be Yvette and her crazy talk, but Lexy couldn't seem to shake the ridiculous, romantic notion of Drew out of her brain, even though the realistic side of her knew it was futile.

A relationship wasn't even on her radar. Her time was consumed by work and therapy and fitness and friends and…life. The life of solitude she'd built, post-prom-night accident. But there he stood in the dappled sunlight…all golden hair and unassuming hotness, and she couldn't just attribute this pull she felt simply to Yvette's offhand comment. Or to the fact that she adored his precious son.

This felt like more. And that terrified her.

She needed to…understand her uncharacteristic fear. To embrace it, remember why she lived the way she did. So she watched. Simply watched.

Sitting next to him and Ian during the ceremony had been a perfect distance to secretly indulge in that omnipresent zing of awareness that shallowed her breathing. But, horrifically, she'd been up on that stage on display, too, with a whole group of nosy, albeit well-meaning, friends—not to mention the entire nosy, albeit well-meaning, town—watching her closely. She couldn't very well have let her curiosity about Drew show then. Nightmare.

Now, though, she wanted to really study him. To see him. To figure out what it was that tangled her up in unfamiliar feelings of shyness and doubt, that left her distracted, disconcerted, dreaming, distraught.

How had he managed to crack her protective shell, when no other man had in all these years? No one since...Randy.

I'm not ready for this.

I'll never be ready for this.

She smacked a lock of hair out of her face.

She'd pegged Drew as shy when they'd met in the hospital, but perhaps she'd been wrong. Sure, he hadn't injected himself into Troublesome Gulch "society," such as it was, but he seemed at ease now. The light breeze fluttered his shirt, outlining his lean torso for a moment before the air shifted, teasing the fabric away from his body. Lexy's chest tightened.

He stood, just in front of Ian, shaking hands and conversing jovially with one of the cops and a couple of paramedics. As he spoke, his hand drifted back and touched Ian's head, as if making sure he was there—absentminded affection, a daddy's instinctual protection.

Damn. Lexy melted. Such a sweet gesture, really. A long sigh escaped her lips before she could stop it. Seriously, was there anything sexier in the world than a devoted father?

And when had she started thinking *that* way?

As if knowing she needed a distraction, Ian crept up to the table and, with a single guilty glance flickered toward his daddy, grabbed a second piece of cake. He was so intent on getting that corner piece, Ian didn't see her. But her eyes tightened with worry as she watched him.

The ceremony had been stimulation enough. Now, after copious doses of sugar and sunshine, Ian looked so wound up, even Lexy could sense an impending meltdown. If he didn't get a nap and some decent food in his belly, not necessarily in that order, the storm was imminent.

He was three bites into his second piece of cake, the hero medal around his neck glinting in the sun as he spun around like little kids hyped on sugar often do. His expression, while animated enough, was tinged with exhaustion, his eyes doggedly glazed. Part of her yearned to call out to him, ask how he was feeling, settle him down on her lap, but she was in no position, nor had she any right, to mother anyone. Another part wanted to alert Drew, in case he hadn't noticed. Not her place.

Instead, she forced herself to keep her nose out of it and know it would be fine. Fine, fine, fine. She wasn't Ian's watcher and didn't even want to start down that mental track. That way lay danger, the kind she couldn't bear to touch. They'd probably leave soon, the grand hero adventure would be over and all the town residents would return to their regularly scheduled lives.

Including her.

Including Drew.

As well it should be.

But, for today…she yearned to be near them. Nearer than she'd managed. Drew and Ian had held full court with most of the Gulch's residents throughout the reception. She'd hardly had any time alone with them.

She stopped just short of a pout, because she wasn't exactly inserting herself into the mix, but it was a combination of relief and letdown to think that this whole stupid fantasy was ending. She was fully aware of how fickle that made her sound. Still…so anticlimactic. Then again, what had she expected?

She pondered the question.

Truth? She wanted more. More…what? More time?

She worried her bottom lip between her teeth.

This sucked. She simply wasn't used to feeling so off-kilter. She was the steady one in her circle of friends, dammit. Ask any of them. But there were parts of her life that set her apart, no getting around it. She'd adapted to them just fine, but she'd never considered…romance. She'd never had to come clean about the wounds of her past, because most everyone in the Gulch already knew.

And even if that wasn't an issue, other obstacles stood in her way. She had plenty of friends with spinal cord injuries who had healthy, loving relationships. But what experience did she have? A high-school romance and the pall of what she'd done hanging over her head? Not a very strong bedrock on which to build anything.

Which is why she remained alone.

Alone was best.

And then Drew had come along and filled her head with crazy thoughts.

Drew was laughing in that deep, rumbling tone she'd begun to recognize in a crowd, when he did a double take toward Ian. The boy was in midreach for cake slice number three, mouth still full of the final bite of piece two.

"Hey, hey. Enough cake, pal." Drew's biceps bulged as he scooped Ian up, just as the boy licked the last bit of frosting off his tiny thumb.

Ian was adorable. Lexy was kind of stuck

on Drew's biceps, though. Her throat tightened on a swallow. As an athlete herself, she appreciated a well-toned body. Clearly the man used his own gym. But that wasn't the problem here.

She knew a lot of men with great physiques, and none of them affected her like Drew had. So…what was it? She was honest enough to admit she was attracted to this man. Like a woman is to a man. She just didn't know how to make it go away, because she sure as hell didn't plan on pursuing it.

"Let's get some real food in your tummy and a nap before I live to regret it," Drew said to his son.

Great minds think alike. Lexy snickered softly, and Drew turned and cocked an eyebrow at her.

She shook her head, lifted the sunglasses to the top of her head. "I didn't mean to eavesdrop. It's nothing. I'd just thought the same thing—food and downtime in short order, or else—"

"Meltdown?"

"Exactly."

"You have good kid instincts," he said. They shared a conspiratorial smile that held just a little longer than necessary. Changed into something that made Lexy's pulse tick at her throat.

No, no, no. This attraction couldn't possibly be mutual. That would kill her.

Maybe it was just her overactive imagination. *Thanks, Yvette.*

A sniffle dragged them back to the matter at hand: Ian, overstimulated, oversugared, over-tired and really just a little boy at the end of the day. His chin quivered.

"Daddy, I don't wanna leave. Everybody's here. I'm havin' fun."

"I know, pal," Drew said gently, cradling the boy's cheek against his shoulder. "But it's past lunchtime."

"I ate."

"The cake doesn't count. Might as well have injected you with pure cane sugar."

Ian's bottom lip sucked in and out, as if he were about to bust into sobs. Drew chucked his chin. "Hey now, you're the hero here. Superman doesn't cry, right?"

"R-right." Ian visibly tried to rein it in.

"How about we go out for lunch?"

"Where?"

Drew pressed his lips into a line, clearly thinking.

"I don't know if you've been there, but the Pinecone's got a great lunch menu," Lexy suggested, gesturing to the far end of the square. "I mean, if you're looking for options. I'm sure they'd love to have a real live hero dining there."

Ian tucked his head deeper into his father's shoulder. "I won't go unless Miss Lexy comes with us," he muttered.

Lexy's heart jumped. She didn't want to look too eager, but lunch with the two of them would be the perfect opportunity for some explainable alone time with Drew. To figure out this unsettling emotional onslaught and release it, once and for all.

Drew rested his cheek on his son's head, rocking him gently. His gaze met Lexy's, and he smiled softly. "Here's a tip for the future of your success with girls, kiddo. You can't demand that a lady eat with you. You have to invite her politely."

Ian raised his head. "Miss Lexy? Come to lunch."

Lexy and Drew laughed. "Good start for now. We'll work on your delivery when you're a little older," Drew told him. He glanced at Lexy. "Don't feel obligated, but we'd love to have you."

Was it her imagination, or had his voice gone husky on that last part? Her lips opened. Nothing emerged.

"Our treat," Drew quickly added. "As a token of our gratitude for all your help."

Ah. A payback lunch. Okay, fair enough. That seemed safe. Better, actually. A little of the spark dimmed inside her, but she was the one determined to fight this attraction. She bestowed as serene a smile as she could. "I'd love to come along." She flicked a glance toward the courthouse lot. "Can I meet you there? I'd like to drive over and park a little closer."

Drew cocked his head in question.

She twisted her mouth, feeling the heat rising up her chest, then indicated the sidewalks. "The city hasn't fixed the buckled concrete on the paths from last year's blizzard. And believe me, I've squawked about it. It's just…easier to drive than maneuver around them."

She registered a look of…alarm? Dismay? Something discomfiting on Drew's face. He recovered quickly, but still, she wondered what he'd been thinking. Frankly, she didn't want to give him constant reminders that she moved through the world differently, of *why* she did. And that bothered her. She hadn't been conscious of her condition since the rehabilitation center, and she hadn't had nightmares about the accident regularly for years. Until this week. Every night.

She wasn't about to fall back into that snake pit of torment over a man she'd never have.

Okay, wait. This was getting idiotic. It was lunch at the Pinecone, not a marriage proposal. And a payback lunch at that. Not even a *date.*

Not even *close* to a date.

She didn't *want* a date! Did she? Oh, God. She sort of did. But she couldn't. She just…*couldn't.* She clutched the hand rims of her chair.

"You okay, Lexy?" Drew asked.

"Yes. Sorry." She shook off the distracting thoughts. "I've probably had too much sun."

He paled. "Are you…sick?"

"I'm fine. I'll meet you over there, okay?"

"Sure." His Adam's apple rose and fell on a thick swallow. "We'll grab a booth."

She spun to leave, oddly disconcerted. This touch and go, unexpected obsession with a man after years of nada, complicated by the added obstacle of her injury and her all-consuming guilt, flat-out sucked. She was thirty-one years old and didn't know how to do…*this,* whatever it was. She didn't even know if she *wanted* to do it. And she sure as hell didn't want to ask her friends about it.

God, talk about wishy-washy.

A feeling of futility settled over her as she

made her way to her minivan. By the time she'd transferred into the driver's seat, her chair stowed in the back, she'd come to the only decision she could handle at this point in her confusion. She'd go to lunch, but after that she'd end this silly, distracting notion of romance and refocus on her therapy, treatments and career. Who needed a man anyway?

Lexy fired up the ignition and backed out of her parking spot. She had a soft spot in her heart for little Ian, no doubt, and would've enjoyed spending time with him. But he'd already become so attached to her, and she didn't want to nurture that. It wasn't safe and it wasn't smart, because in the end, she'd have to disappear.

So, she'd be just another Gulcher to Drew and Ian. Her life was just fine the way she'd built it.

Lexy made Drew want to change his life. There it was. He'd shied away from it, but as they sat across from each other in the quaint little diner, as he looked in her eyes, as they shared getting-to-know-you conversation over coffee, he knew. She wasn't just some woman his friends hoped to hook him up with to get him "over" Gina's death. Lexy Cabrera was something special. She was a woman who cared about herself, her community, her friends. She was the absolute opposite of Gina, in all the ways that counted. Someone he'd love to spend more time with.

They'd discussed her job, the incredible—in his mind—things she'd done with 9-1-1. All the saves, all the people helped. Did she even realize how amazing she was? He only wished Ian were hearing it all.

Ian, however, was splayed out in the booth and snoozing hard before the food even arrived. But, as far as Drew was concerned, sleep took precedence over eating at this point. He brushed his son's hair back from his face, suffused with a love so big it stole his breath. It had always been this way watching him sleep, so innocent and vulnerable.

Did Lexy love children?

Did she ever think about raising a child?

It certainly seemed like it. Drew closed his eyes for a moment. He was getting way ahead of himself, falling under Lexy's spell just like Ian had.

"Will you wake him when the food comes?" Lexy asked softly, her elbows propped on the edge of the table, those gorgeous, slanted green eyes focused on Ian.

Drew shook his head. "This kid always wakes up grouchy and hungry, which is something you don't want to see, trust me. I'll let him sleep off the grouch and feed him later." And, frankly, he looked forward to talking to Lexy more without worrying that Ian would steal the show or ask an embarrassing question. They'd gotten past the small talk, the work talk, and now he wanted to really get to know this woman. He may have been reading too much into it, but she'd seemed pensive at the awards reception. Why? Worth a try to find out, but he got the sense he needed to ease into it. He sipped his coffee. "So, tell me about your racing."

Lexy cocked her head to the side. "My racing?"

He shrugged. "I'm a bit of a jock. What can I say?"

She smiled gently. "Well, I started out with five-K races, just to keep fit, and now I'm up to half marathons and triathlons. I have a race coming up in White Peaks. Do you know where that is?"

"I do."

"I'm training pretty hard for that. It takes a lot of upper-body strength to go that long. So I lift. Swim. Swimming is my favorite."

"Yeah? Why's that?"

She hesitated, and her eyes darkened with

what looked like worry. "Have you ever known someone with a spinal cord injury, Drew?"

"No, I haven't."

She wrapped her hands around her mug. "In the water, I feel free. Fully able-bodied. Powerful. I cut through the water with my own body strength, and that's…something."

His stomach coiled with respect and, strangely, desire. He did wonder what kind of romantic life Lexy had, or wanted. That was conversation for a much, much later time. "I can understand that," he said.

She held up a hand. "Please don't misunderstand. People often view my way of life with pity—"

"I never—"

"Not you," she assured him. "That's not what I meant. But, if we're going to be…friends, you need to understand." She lowered her chin and leveled him with a gaze. "I get the feeling you walk on eggshells around my condition a lot."

"I'm sorry about that. I just don't want to offend."

"It's okay, but you need to stop worrying about offending me." She gazed past him, seeming to weigh her words. "The thing is, I'm lucky, Drew. I'm alive. Not everyone from my accident is."

"Ah, Lexy. I'm so sorry."

She dropped her gaze, and the look of pain that swept across her face made him want to hold her. "I'm fully independent. Strong. Healthy. And I take care of myself."

He was glad to hear that.

"My chair isn't a prison, like most walking people imagine. It's…freedom to me. You move through the world on two legs. Me? On two wheels. Other than that, there are no differences between us. Well…other than the obvious. You being a man and me being—"

"A woman," he said, surprised at how sensual the words sounded on his lips.

Clearly Lexy caught it, too, because a blush rose to her cheeks. "Exactly." She swallowed carefully. "Do you understand what I'm saying?"

"I think so. I don't mean to treat you as if you're fragile. You're clearly strong. Fit. More fit than most people I know."

A small smile teased up the corners of her mouth, and it tightened his jaw. "I try. Thank you. It helps with daily life, too, keeping fit. I'm able to do just about anything I want or need without help."

He'd ask her more about that later. Drew intertwined his fingers and propped them under his chin. "So, where do you train?"

Lexy laughed, and the husky sound twirled straight down to his lower abdomen and settled, tight and hot. This woman didn't have a high-pitched giggle. No sirree. She laughed with a deep sexiness that perfectly matched her dark, sultry, pinup-girl looks.

"Is this a sales pitch for your gym?" she teased.

"No, no, of course not. It's...well, to be honest, it might've been a pitch. Would love to have you there." He smiled, hoping it looked as sheepish as he felt.

"Thank you. I'll stop by sometime. I swim at the high school every day, and I actually get regular PT and train with a wonderful therapist, Kimberly, at the hospital, in the sports rehab wing. Cagney's husband—"

"Jonas, right?"

"Wow, you're good with names. Especially considering you got hit with tons of them today. Anyway, yeah. Jonas is one of the biggest bene-factors for High Country Medical Center, and he tricked out the rehabilitation room with training machines I could only have dreamed about be-fore. He's a good guy, such a good friend."

"Sounds like it. I'd love to see the rehab room."

He flipped his hand at the inquisitive tilt of her head. "I was a coach in Virginia. Before… I have a thing about tricked-out training rooms."

"Well, then you should stop by."

"I will."

"What did you coach?"

"Track and field. I have a few athletes who went on to the Olympics after college."

"Wow. That had to be hard to give up."

Drew shot a glance at Ian. "It was worth it, for him. Too many ghosts in the old house. Too many memories, and not all of them good."

"I understand that, believe me."

They fell silent for a moment while their food was delivered. "Here you go, Lex. And, Drew, isn't it?" the waitress asked.

"Yes, it is. Thanks. Looks great."

The waitress hiked her chin. "And the little guy there? That's the newest Gulch hero, right?"

"Sure is," Lexy said.

"Ian," Drew added.

The older woman indicated his kiddie meal. "Safe to assume you want me to box this up for Mister Ian?"

"That would be great." Drew smiled.

After she left, Lexy picked up her fork and dug in to her food. Drew stilled, fork halfway between plate and mouth. Was there anything sexier than a woman who wasn't afraid to hit a meal with gusto? Lexy was no half-size salad woman, and he appreciated that more than she knew.

She looked up while chewing and caught him staring. Her eyebrows raised. She swallowed and dabbed at her lips with her napkin. "Starving, sorry. Is your food okay?" she asked, glancing at his untouched plate.

"Oh. It's great." He took a bite as if to prove his words true.

"Drew?" She paused, twirled her fork in thought. "Now that I've blathered on about my life, is it okay to ask you about Ian's mom? About what happened? Or is that still too fresh a hurt?"

"No. It's…fine. It's been two years, Lexy. Like I said, Ian and I moved here to start over." He quirked his mouth to the side. "The little guy's having an easier time jumping on that goal than I am, I'm afraid. I don't intend to be a hermit forever. I just don't want him to be hurt again." Did he imagine it, or had she paled?

"Of course not."

"He has nightmares. Wets the bed some nights. It breaks my heart. And he really misses having a woman in his life."

"Poor baby," she said, her troubled gaze on

Ian. But she'd definitely paled. What was that about?

Drew straightened his flatware and situated the napkin on his lap. Shored up his composure. "Anyway, Gina was diabetic. From childhood." He twisted his lips with regret. "Unfortunately, instead of managing her condition, living with it, she chose to laugh in its face. Problem was the disease got the last laugh."

"God." Lexy widened her eyes. "I'm so sorry."

He nodded. "It was a point of contention throughout our entire marriage, her absolute recklessness with her health, even knowing she had a son who needed her." Why had he said that? Flooded with regret, he pressed his lips flat. "I shouldn't have said that," he bit off. "I don't mean to disparage her or sound resentful." He glanced guiltily at Ian.

To his surprise, Lexy reached across the table and covered his hand with one of her own, which seemed a bit shaky. "It's okay. I know you didn't mean anything by it." She squeezed once, then released his fingers.

He missed the feel of her warm skin on his. And besides, he *had* meant something by it. He had loved Gina, for sure. She was the mother of his son. But he harbored a bubbling pot of anger over the way she'd chosen to deal with her diabetes, how little regard it seemed to show for her son. Her young son who needed her.

"I hate recklessness. That's the thing. She and I had always planned on having a big family, but she couldn't even take care of herself for one child." He blew out a breath. "When she fell into the diabetic coma that day…we found her. Ian and I. After an afternoon hike. I can't—" he shook his head "—can't seem to evict that horrible image from my brain."

"I…I understand," Lexy said, her voice wavering. She set down her fork with a bit of a clatter. "Would you…excuse me for a moment? I'm just going to run to…" She indicated the sign for the restrooms.

"No, sure. Go ahead," Drew said, standing as she prepared to leave the table. "Is everything okay?"

"Of course. Yes," she said, not sounding truthful, as she escaped as fast as possible. "I'll be right back."

Once she was gone, the air seemed to have left the room. Drew sat and blew out a breath. Clearly he'd said something, done something. But what? Should he have left out his feelings about Gina's death? Lexy had simply asked what happened, not for a list of complaints about his marriage, a rant against a dead woman. *Idiot.*

He combed all ten fingers through his hair and wondered if he'd ever get this right.

Chapter Seven

Lexy locked herself in the small restroom and took several deep breaths to slow her heartbeat. If she'd thought her prospects for any kind of relationship with Drew were sketchy before, they'd just tumbled into the impossible realm. The one thing he couldn't handle? Recklessness.

How perfect was that?

If it weren't so damn sad, she'd laugh.

The very trait that had changed the course of her life was the one thing he couldn't handle. And it wasn't as if she could hide what had happened, or take it back. The whole world knew. Her body was a physical reminder of it every day, and the truth was bound to come out sooner or later in any kind of honest relationship, which would mean there *was* no relationship. No. No setting herself up for failure. That wasn't her style. She needed to cut her losses, thank Drew for lunch and escape back to comfortable reality. Now.

Moving wearily to the sink, Lexy splashed her face with ice-cold water and dried it on a rough, brown paper towel, appreciating the chafing pain, the raw smell of the paper pulp. She stared at herself in the ancient mirror, hardly recognizing the woman staring back at her. She looked…ravaged. And she didn't like herself this way. All this brought about by an attraction to a man?

"No more," she whispered. It wasn't worth it.

She couldn't put herself in the position to get hurt, and she couldn't allow Drew or Ian to relive any of the pain they'd experienced with Gina's death.

But how to make a quick exit? After a moment, Lexy pulled her cell phone out of her side pocket and dialed. Genean answered on the second ring.

"Troublesome Gulch Communications, Genean speaking."

"Hey, G, it's Lex."

"Hey! What's up, boss? How'd the hero thing go?"

"It was fine. Listen, I need a favor."

"Name it."

Lexy pressed her eyes closed, the sadness closing in and making her claustrophobic. "Call me in two minutes and tell me I'm needed at work, okay?"

"Um, sure, if you want. But we're fine here."

Lexy shook her head and actually smiled through her pain. "I realize that, hon. You're doing me a favor, remember? It's not real. I'm not actually going to come there."

"Oh. Right! I'm getting you out of a situation." Genean laughed, and Lexy appreciated the younger woman's ability to laugh at herself without feeling the least bit self-conscious. She was a bit of a ditz, but an endearing one. "Okay, two minutes."

"Thanks." Lexy disconnected, straightened her shoulders and pasted on a happy face. Satisfied she could pull it off, she unlocked the door and headed back toward the table.

Drew caught sight of her and stood as she

approached. Something about that chivalrous gesture squeezed her heart. Here she was, saying goodbye already, and she'd barely scratched the surface of knowing him. She didn't even know anything about his family. Clearly, he'd been raised to be mannerly. But beyond that...

Did he have siblings?

Did he go all out for the Christmas holidays, or was he more of a bah-humbug sort?

Did he watch reality TV?

Colgate or Crest?

Morning person or night owl?

All those little details she'd never know. *Don't think about it, Lex.* He seemed tense, watchful, until he really got a look at her. Then he relaxed a few levels, which came as a relief. Apparently she was pulling off the happy-go-lucky farce, even though her insides were imploding.

She tossed her hair and flashed a brilliant smile. "Sorry about that. What did I miss?"

"Nothing at all." As he sat, he aimed a thumb at Ian. "That one's still zonked. Are you...okay?"

"Of course. Everything's fine." As if to prove her point, she picked up her fork and started in on her meal again, although the idea of food in her stomach made her ill. She took a gelatinous bite. Her throat protested as she chewed, but she willed herself to appear normal.

"So, I apologize if I gave too much information about what happened with Gina," Drew said.

Lexy shook her head, waving away his concerns as so much nothingness. She swallowed the bite, then took a quick sip of water so she didn't choke on the horror of it all. "Don't apologize. I understand completely, and I don't want you to think—" Her phone rang. She glanced down at her side pocket. "Excuse me just a moment. I wouldn't answer, but that's the work tone, unfortunately."

"On a Saturday?"

She nodded as she pulled the phone from her side pocket. "I'm the boss. I'm on call twenty-four/seven." She held up a finger. "This is Lexy."

"It's me, boss," Genean whispered, as if they were on some spy mission.

"Hey, what's going on?"

"Um…nothing? Hello, you told me to call in two minutes, remember?"

Lexy sighed. Genean, bless her heart, did not have a future in covert operations. "How many times did you get the failure indicator?"

"Huh?"

"Okay, yeah, that's not good. Hang tight and I'll be there as soon as I can, okay?"

"Oh, I get it." Genean giggled. "Roger that, double-O-seven. Over and out." The phone went dead.

Lexy made a show of groaning as she put her phone away. "I'm really sorry, Drew. They're having a problem with some of the equipment in the comm center. I have to head over and take care of it."

"Of course. I understand." He held up his palms. "And lunch is our treat, remember."

"Thank you. I had a nice time." She glanced over at Ian, and an unexpected lump rose in her throat. She had to swallow several times to strip the emotion from her words. It all felt so damned final. "Will you tell him I said goodbye?"

"I will. He'll be sad he missed you."

She wanted to say she'd miss him, too. That she'd see him soon. But she couldn't lie. She glanced up at the man who'd been her big fantasy for a week. Fun while it lasted, she supposed. Fun and turbulent. "Goodbye, Drew," she said. Meaning it more literally than he knew.

Days melted into weeks, and before Drew realized it, a full month had passed. A month where he'd neither seen nor spoken to Lexy. Maybe that whole thing had been a stupid fantasy, but he had a niggling fear that he'd said or done something to send her running, and he just couldn't figure it out.

He'd spent the lonely month focused on unpacking his belongings, on turning their little ranch house into a home he and Ian could be proud of, but he never stopped thinking about Lexy.

He'd left her a few messages after their apparently disastrous lunch, none of which she returned. He'd sent her and the whole emergency communications center monthlong free passes to his gym under the half guise of thanking them for their work. Well, he *did* appreciate the work they did, but really, he'd hoped to lure Lexy there. A few of the dispatchers had come by. But no Lexy.

Even Ian had stopped talking incessantly about her, but Drew could tell the boy was forlorn, missing her, feeling that pain of loss all over again. It killed Drew. Ian had a picture of himself with Lexy from the hero ceremony propped up on the little table next to his bed, and every time Drew saw that, it chipped a little piece of his heart. That made his need to reconnect with Lexy even more important. If she had no interest in him, he would learn to deal with it. But Ian adored her, and he was too young to understand why Miss Lexy wasn't their friend.

Drew stood out on the back deck, sipping coffee and looking out over the Rocky Mountains range that cupped his property. He had made a promise to Ian to throw a housewarming party, and he meant to keep it. If any house needed to be warmed, it was this one. But he had to make damn sure Lexy would show.

So, he decided to call in reinforcements.

Brody's business card was in the outside pocket of Drew's backpack, just where it had been since the day on Deer Track Trailhead. He fished the slip of paper out and studied it. Wrinkled, tattered, but an invitation nonetheless, and one without an expiration date.

The phone rang three times before Brody picked up.

"Hey, it's Drew Kimball." He could hear Brody's baby daughter crying in the background. "Is this a bad time?"

"No, not at all. Let me just step outside to get away from the noise. Hang on."

Drew listened to heavy footsteps, a door creaking open, and then the sounds of the crying ceased. "Drew, man. Good to hear from you. I wondered where you'd up and disappeared to over the past month."

"Believe it or not," Drew said wryly, "I was under pressure from a six-year-old to finish unpacking our boxes so we could throw a party for our new friends. A housewarming party."

Brody laughed. "Hey, I understand. When I moved here, I bought a furnished house. Nothing special, but fine for a guy alone. Lived in the musty, old, decrepit place happily until Faith came along and forced me to redecorate. Actually, she did it herself."

Drew's thoughts drifted to Lexy. What was her house like? "Bet it was nice to have a woman's touch."

"That's the truth." Brody paused. "So what's up?"

"Well, it's about the housewarming party. I want to set a date, maybe get your help inviting some people? You and Faith, the others."

"Sure thing. Our circle would love to come."

"But before that, I'm wondering if you, Nate and Jonas would have time to help me build a ramp to the front door. I'd like the place to be accessible—"

"For Lex."

He blew out a breath. "Yeah." He wasn't sure

whether or not to show his hand here. "Ian would be crushed if she couldn't come."

A beat passed. "And what about you?"

"Me?"

"I gotta say, the rest of us thought there might be something brewing between you and Lex."

Screw it. He needed to confide in someone. "The truth? I'd be crushed, too, if she didn't show. As for the rest, Lexy made it pretty clear she has zero interest in any sort of relationship with me."

"How so?"

"Bailed on a lunch, hasn't returned a single phone message. Never used her free pass to the gym. I haven't seen her once around town."

"Don't take that to mean anything. These Gulch women, bro, I have to say." Brody whistled low. "Tough cases. Except for Faith. She took the lead in our relationship. But, Cagney? Erin? Lexy? Expect some resistance."

Their whole circle of friends, Drew realized. It wasn't the women in Troublesome Gulch, it was the women who made up Lexy's closest friends. But why? He'd mull over that later. "Resistance I'd take. She flat out hasn't spoken to me in a month."

"Well, we'll fix that. I'll gather the guys. How

about we start this Saturday? We ought to be able to knock out a ramp in a few sessions with four of us working."

"Sounds great. Food and beer are on me."

"Say no more. As for the party, I know for a fact Lexy is off work a month from Saturday, because we're all going to Cagney's for her monthly dinner party."

A deep yearning coiled around Drew. After living as a loner for so long, it surprised him how much he'd love to be included in their inner circle.

Oblivious to Drew's turmoil, Brody added, "But I'm sure I can convince Cag to divert next month's party to your place. It's for a good cause, a housewarming. Plus, we've been trying to pull Lexy out of her shell for a long time now. She's something special."

"Definitely special." Drew frowned. "But she doesn't strike me as the type to have a shell."

A pause stretched and crackled over the phone line. "How much do you know about the accident? The one where she was injured?"

"Not much. Just that it was a car accident."

Brody pulled in a long breath and blew it out. "Well, I'll let her tell it when she's ready. It's her story, not mine. But trust me, there are all different kinds of shells." He cleared his throat. "So, Saturday works?"

"We'll plan on that. Hey, Brody?"

"Yeah?"

"Thanks."

"What are friends for?"

The two best things about swimming laps in the morning? No one else was at the pool, and the water masked tears. She'd been shedding a lot of those over the past month. Lexy thought she'd get over the dream of Drew and Ian immediately, but the more she avoided them, the sadder she felt. How had a little boy and his widowed father managed to affect her so deeply?

Her tears had mixed with the chlorinated water for the last four laps. As she turned and sliced her way through the water for the final lap, unfamiliar underwater sounds caught her attention.

Splash! Splunk! Splash!

She lifted her head as she reached the wall and came face-to-face with none other than Cagney, Erin and Faith. Grappling through the water, she white-knuckled the wall.

"God, you scared me. What on earth are you guys doing here?" she asked, breathing heavily.

She pushed wet locks of hair away from her forehead.

"Lex," Erin said. "You've been avoiding everyone. You need to talk about this."

The other two nodded.

Lexy's heart thrummed. She'd been on the other side of these friend-interventions before, but never the subject of one. "Talk about what? Swimming? I swim every day. You know that."

"You're so distant, and we understand it's probably because we're pushy and nosy. But why are you acting like you never met Ian? Or Drew?" Cagney asked softly. "He really seems to like you."

"I'm not avoiding Drew," Lexy sputtered, looking away. "I hardly know the man. Just because of...of the hero thing. He's not a part of my life."

"But that's your choice," Erin said.

Water lapped against the blue tile of the pool as the four of them bobbed in the shallow end.

"He's called you several times. You told me," Faith said. "But you haven't called him back."

"How do you know I haven't?" she asked, narrowing her gaze and looking from friend to friend. They exchanged knowing glances with each other.

"Because Brody, Nate and Jonas are all at his house right now," Faith said.

"They are?" Surprise blew through Lexy like a cool wind. It felt almost awkward that her friends had all welcomed Drew in while she'd done just the opposite. But it shouldn't have. It wasn't as if she had any claim over him. "Why?"

The three friends encircled her. Faith shivered and ducked down to her neck to grow accustomed to the temperature. Cagney splashed water on her shoulders.

"They're having a housewarming party next month—Drew and Ian," Erin said. "And Drew wanted help building a ramp so his place is accessible."

A little part of Lexy melted. Another little part died and blew away like so much ash. She couldn't keep her tears back. "Oh. Oh, no. Please tell me he's not."

"Why is that a bad thing, hon?" Erin asked.

But Lexy couldn't say. She shook her head.

"You have to go to the party," Cagney said. "That's the thing. We're all going there instead of to my place for next month's dinner party, so I know you're not working. But, let's face it, he doesn't truly care if all of us go. He wants you there."

"Ian does, too," Faith added. "He showed Brody a photograph of the two of you at the hero ceremony. He keeps it by his bed. So whatever it is, spit it out. You're our friend. We're here for you."

Lexy sucked in a sniffle. "You guys just don't understand. I'm not right for Drew and Ian. It'll never work and I'm…I'm not ready."

Faith clucked with sympathy, then swished through the water next to her and wrapped her arm around Lexy's shoulders. "What are you afraid of?"

"I'm not afraid. I'm realistic. I don't want… to hurt them."

"Now, how could you possibly hurt them?" Erin asked, confusion in her eyes.

Lexy gulped back a sob and shook her head, her lips pressed together. "I don't…need—I don't want to date. Please understand. It's too much. Too terrifying."

"But how could you hurt them?" Erin insisted.

"If it's not right, Erin, that little boy will lose another female in his life. I'm not sure I want to be responsible for that kind of pain."

"You know we just want you to be happy, Lex," Cagney said. "Whatever that means. If that means you're alone by choice, we honor that. Right?"

Erin and Faith nodded.

"But it needs to be a choice for a good reason. I mean, look at us." Cagney lifted her arms wide in the water. "We all went through hell to get where we are now. I never thought I'd have Jonas back."

"But she does," Faith said. "And I have Brody. Erin has Nate. Love isn't always easy."

"I'm not in love!"

"Maybe not, but you have to put yourself out there if you ever want to find it," Erin said. "You're an amazing woman, and you have a six-year-old boy attached to you. Wondering why you're not a part of his life. We're just saying, you should talk to Drew. At least help him understand why you disappeared from his and Ian's world for no reason they can figure out."

"And you should come to the housewarming party," Cagney added. "You can't miss that."

Lexy sniffed, wiping ineffectually at her tears with her wet hands. "He's seriously building a ramp?"

"Right at this moment." Cagney lowered her chin.

"Why would he do that?"

"Wow, this chick needs stuff spelled out. Speak slowly, use one-syllable words. Because, doofus, he wants you to cross it and enter his house. His world," Faith said. "He's reaching out, Lex."

"You really think so? It's worth the risk?"

"Yes. But the next step's up to you."

Chapter Eight

Lexy arrived in the rehab room at the hospital twenty minutes early for her regular session with Kimberly. This place felt like a second home to her, and she used the downtime to think, to listen to her saved messages from Drew. To try and figure out what exactly she'd say when she called.

Her friends said he was worth the risk, but she needed to figure out how to make things up to him before she ever made that leap. If she intended to go to the housewarming party next month, she needed to make amends long before that. Only, she couldn't come up with a great way to bridge that gap between their lunch and all the weeks she had ignored him.

How to explain?

Her friends had been right. But she was done lying to herself. She did want to get to know Drew, but thanks to her fear, she'd really screwed things up. "Such an idiot," she muttered, shoving her hands into padded workout gloves and pressing them closed over the backs of her wrists.

She stretched, then warmed up with some overzealous, lightweight lat pull-downs. After that she moved toward the wall mirrors and rolled one shoulder, then the next, to loosen them. Her muscles were soon warm and relaxed, but inside tension coiled as tightly as a spring ready to break.

How long had she been this way?

So tense? So afraid of risk?

Since the accident? And how much longer could she stand it? She reached for her Lofstrand crutches propped against the wall, secured them on her arms, then pulled herself into a standing position. She stared at herself in the mirror, scrutinized the image before her. Strangely enough— or not—she looked no different to herself standing or sitting. She was the same Lexy she'd ever known, walking or not. None of that made an impact on who she was, what she'd done. Blowing out a breath, she closed her eyes, and her stomach fluttered with the single thought…

Drew built a ramp.

To his house. His life.

The man built a ramp.

And after that she'd basically blown him off.

How could she let him know how touched she was by the gesture when she was so…scared? Scared of what he'd think when she told him about her past? Scared he'd be okay with it. Scared he wouldn't.

Scared she could really fall for the guy….

And ashamed because she'd been too damn scared to show him even common courtesy.

Just then, Kimberly bopped into the room, a whirlwind of healthy energy, and shrugged her duffel bag off her shoulder. It hit the hard rubber floor with a soft *thunk*. "Hey, sweetie! You're here early. And you're up! Good. Let's get you on the treadmill. You want to walk there, or—?"

Lexy shook her head in amusement at the perky, pony-tailed blonde. "I'm a little tired today. I think I'll conserve energy and use my chair if that's okay."

"Whatever works."

Kimberly bounced over to the LiteGait partial-body-weight treadmill, a training gem Jonas had purchased for the rehab room. She set things up while Lexy returned to her chair and made her way across the room. Lexy had always wished for a LiteGait, which was doing wonders for her strength and stamina. She couldn't ever thank Jonas enough. Sometimes, with all the access she had to therapeutic equipment and a trainer like Kimberly, she felt like she actually might walk again someday.

If she wanted to.

But she'd begun to realize her heart needed healing more than her limbs.

This room, and Kimberly's diligent study of spinal cord injury research, made her feel as if she could accomplish anything. Anything, that is, except forgiving herself.

And accepting love.

But Drew had built a ramp. A ramp! That truly meant something. He might not have meant it this way, but she took it as an acceptance of her different abilities, and she appreciated it more than she even knew how to express. She had the opportunity to reach out toward romance, toward Drew, and maybe eventually find love, if only she could master the self-forgiveness part.

She sighed as Kimberly helped secure her into the harness, then engaged the hydraulic lift to raise Lexy gently upright and into a steady position. Lexy braced herself on the arm bars.

"Comfortable?" Kimberly asked.

"Yep."

Kimberly pushed some buttons and Lexy's body started walking, in spite of its limitations. The magic of technology. "The speed good?"

"Uh-huh."

"Any pain anywhere?"

Just my heart. "Nope."

"So, what was the big sigh about, Lex?"

Lexy cast her a sidelong glance. She should've known better than to sigh in front of Kimberly. "You caught that, huh?"

Kimberly crinkled her face into an expression of sympathy. "Kind of hard to miss. Also out of character for you. And it seems as if you've been this way for a few weeks now, if you want the truth."

A few weeks? Lexy considered that. "It is out of character, isn't it? I'm a happy person. I've always been a happy person."

"So, what changed?"

I saw the possibility of a future with a man. Lexy warred with herself. Should she talk about it? Though Kimberly was a dear friend, she wasn't in Lexy's nosy, matchmaking inner circle. It might do her good to have an objective opinion. "Kim? How do you know when it's time to take a risk on someone, regardless of what you have to give up? How do you know when to take a chance on…love?"

To her surprise, Kimberly paled. She banged the side of her fist against the body of the machine. "Oh, no. Dammit! I knew the stupid TG grapevine would get me. I was going to wait until after the session to talk to you. I mean, I just found out yesterday. Who told you?"

Lexy blinked in confusion. Weren't they talking about her and Drew? "Told me what?"

"That…that I'm leaving, silly. What else?" The therapist flashed a pristine diamond solitaire on the third finger of her left hand.

"Oh, my God."

"Yeah, Bruce finally coughed up the rock. Can you believe it? And since his residency is in Boston—" a look of horrified realization came over Kimberly's face as she no doubt caught the trembling in Lexy's chin. Kim pressed her palms to the sides of her own face. "Wait. Oh, no. No. We're talking about two different things, aren't we?"

Hot tears stung the back of Lexy's eyelids. At least someone was in love. "I think we are, Kimberly, but I'm suddenly far more interested in what you have to say."

Kimberly's expression fell. "You hadn't heard?"

"No."

"And I blew it."

Lexy's emotions were too edgy. Unexpectedly, she burst into tears, covering her eyes with one hand. Why had she been crying so much lately? Not only was she happy by nature, but she was the calm, collected type. It was part of what made her so good at her job. Calm, collected, that is until Drew Kimball blew into town.

"Lexy. It's okay."

"You're seriously leaving the Gulch?"

"I am. I have to follow my heart. I'm so sorry."

Lexy stumbled slightly on the machine, and Kimberly immediately powered it down so Lexy wouldn't get hurt. Once it had come to a full stop, Lexy searched the other woman's eyes. "When?"

"God, I never intended to spring it on you like this."

"No. No. Don't be ridiculous. I'm so happy for you," Lexy said, in a watery, blubbery tone that completely belied her words. She reached for Kimberly's hand and inspected the ring. "You deserve this happiness. You've wanted this for so long."

"Thank you." Kimberly helped lower her back down into her chair, then implored her, "But you deserve it, too, Lex. When are you going to grab for your happiness?"

Lexy waved the question away, not wanting to even dip her toes in the swamp of her own discontent anymore. It hardly seemed relevant. She wasn't going to taint Kimberly's news with her own crap. Kimberly had been waiting for Bruce to pop the question as long as Lexy had known her. Of course, he'd been in medical school, but still. "This is about you. Your special moment." She shook her hair back and struggled to brighten. "I assume I'll be invited to the wedding?"

"Of course." The two women beamed at each other, although Lexy's chin still quivered.

"When do you leave?" she asked softly.

Kimberly glanced wistfully around the rehab room. "You want to finish our workout first?"

"No, I can't. Just tell me." Lexy bit her bottom lip, bracing herself for the worst.

Kimberly took a deep breath in, then let it out. "Two weeks."

"Oh, God." Lexy's hands shook. She pulled the Velcro closures apart and peeled her lifting gloves off the tips of her fingers, then dropped the gloves to the floor.

"Please don't worry," Kimberly pleaded, sounding worried herself. "They're going to hire another therapist. Anyone would be lucky to work with you, and in this amazing facility." She widened her arms as if taking it all in.

"Yeah, but he or she won't be you. You've been the best, most inspiring trainer."

Kimberly took both of Lexy's hands in her own. "And you've been the most inspiring patient. I'm going to miss you so much. Not just working with you, but your amazing drive and big heart. Most of all, your friendship."

"We'll stay in touch," Lexy said. "You'll always be my friend."

"I know. Now, what was it you asked me before I accidentally blew it with my news?"

"Nothing. It wasn't anything." Lexy sniffed and pulled back. "Can we... Do you mind if we call it a day? It's been a whirlwind couple of weeks, and with this news—even though I'm happy for you—I'm just not up for a workout."

Kimberley's eyes fell into worry. "Do you want to sit and talk?"

Lexy gave her a tremulous smile. "No. I don't want my sadness over losing you to affect your happiness over Bruce or the ring or the wedding or Boston. You should go on and enjoy the day. I'm afraid I'd be poor company."

"You're sure?"

Lexy nodded. "I'm just going to hang out in here for a bit and think. Alone time is just the ticket."

Kimberly stood and looped the strap of her duffel crosswise over her toned body. "But we'll work out together for the next two weeks, yes?"

"Yes. Definitely." Lexy smoothed her palms together. "I just need to absorb the news and I'll be just fine."

Kimberly leaned in and kissed Lexy on the cheek. "Lock up behind you, okay?"

Lexy didn't trust herself to speak, so she nodded again, biting the insides of her cheeks. And with that, her beloved physical rehab therapist and longtime training partner…was gone. She had two weeks to figure out how in the hell she was going to be ready for the first race of the season. Or if she even wanted to bother.

You have to do it.

Her inner voice was right. She'd never been one to stop living when life threw her a curveball. Now wasn't the time to start.

But had she really been living at all?

She toyed with calling her friends for moral support, but as much as she loved them, she couldn't stomach the onslaught. Another idea popped into her head—a crazier idea, but one that made her heart pound.

It could be a brilliant segue. Or it might not work. But what did she have to lose? Her training methods were superspecific to her condition, of course. A lot to consider. But, this could be just the olive branch she'd been searching for.

Reach out for your happiness, Lexy. What do you have to lose? Other than everything...

Drew had no idea what had prompted Lexy's call after so much pointed silence, but he wasn't going to question it. He just wanted to see her, had wanted to see her since the last time. So, when she had asked him to come over to the hospital rehab room, he hadn't hesitated. His employee, Rick, was working at the gym that morning so Drew had time to catch up on paperwork. But Lexy was infinitely more important than paperwork. Nothing would keep him from saying yes to her request.

He was more than a little curious to find out whether or not she'd come clean about the last time they'd seen each other during lunch at the diner. What he'd done or said to kick her into fight-or-flight mode, emphasis on *flight*. Try as he might, he hadn't been able to figure it out.

Following the directions she'd provided, he traversed the polished hallways of High Country Medical Center and, before long, he made a sharp right turn into a rehab room that was so amazing and well-equipped, he had to pause in the doorway and take it all in.

Wow.

He could understand why Lexy chose to work out here instead of his gym. This place could accommodate her needs in a way no mainstream gym ever would. His eyes scanned the LiteGait treadmill and other adaptive equipment with something akin to lust. And then he caught sight of her, standing by the mats with the help of the Canadian crutches she'd told Ian she could use now and then, her chair safely behind her. It was interesting to see her standing, but he found it also didn't matter. She was just as beautiful sitting or standing. She was the same Lexy who made him want to make peace with his past and work on building some kind of a future.

His heart squeezed.

"Hey, stranger," he said, his voice unintentionally husky. She was just…so standout, such a strong, beautiful, determined woman.

Her gaze shot to his, alarm in those gorgeous green eyes. "Drew. Hi."

It was all she said, but hearing his name on her lips ignited a slow burn deep inside. "Long time, no see."

"Yeah…I'm…sorry about that."

He shrugged off her apology. None of that mattered now that they were in the same room together. "This place is unbelievable," he said, crossing the room toward her. "I have equipment envy."

Her lips quivered as she maneuvered back into her chair and set the crutches aside. "It takes a strong man to admit such a thing, Drew, I'll give you that."

They laughed at his unintentional double entendre, although it sounded nervous on both their parts.

Lexy cleared her throat and craned to look past him. "Where's Ian?"

"Staying with the neighbor. I...wanted us to have some time to talk alone." He hiked one shoulder. "It's been a long time, and that kid tends to steal every scene, you know."

"Yes. He's a great little guy." She paused, seemed to shore up her resolve. "I miss him, Drew."

Carefully, not wanting to break the spell, he sat down on a weight bench across from her. He took his time. Now that she'd invited him back into her life, he was going to make damn sure he didn't screw it up again. "You know you're always welcome in our world, Lex. He misses you, too. More than you realize. You're his number-one hero."

"I'm sorry about...letting him down like that." She cut her glance away, picked at an invisible thread on her track pants. "I never meant to just disappear."

"What happened?" he asked softly.

"Oh, Drew." She sighed. "There are things you don't know. Things you should know before...if we were ever to...what I mean to say is—"

"Just tell me."

To his surprise, her gorgeous, slanted eyes were watery when she looked at him. "First, I'm sorry for not returning your calls. I'm not usually rude. I just…"

"Freaked?"

Her gorgeous face fell into a mask of misery. "Yeah. Sort of."

"It's okay. That happens. But, I'm just curious why? Was it something I did? Or said?"

"No, nothing like that. You don't understand."

He moved the bench closer and took one of Lexy's hands in his, absentmindedly smoothing his thumb over her soft knuckles. "Then, help me understand. I really want to."

With a quick, nervous dart of her tongue, she moistened her lips. "I haven't…dated since before the accident."

He nodded. He'd figured that was it.

"But that's not the problem," she said, completely dispelling his previous thought.

Okay, that surprised him. If she wasn't shy about dating or getting to know a man because of her condition… "Then what?"

"The thing is—" her throat worked over a couple of swallows "—I'm a lot more like… Gina…than you know."

Now that wasn't at all what he expected to

hear. From where he stood, Lexy Cabrera was nothing at all like Gina. He blinked a couple times, searching, seeking some sort of similarity. "I don't understand, Lexy. You mean because you both deal with a physical condition?"

"No, no. Worse," she said, almost mournfully. "Way worse. It's the recklessness aspect, I'm afraid."

He frowned. None of this made sense. "I don't follow. You take great care of yourself, Lexy. Gina didn't. That's how Gina was reckless."

"I know. It's not that."

A thought dawned on him as if someone had thrown open a door to the bright Colorado sunlight. "Wait. Is this about your accident?"

She nodded, and the pensiveness returned.

But that was a lifetime ago. "Talk to me about it, Lex. Nothing you could say would change how much I admire and respect you."

"Don't be so sure." Her hand started trembling within his grasp. "But I…actually, I need to talk to you about it, scared or not. I want to. Because, strange as it sounds, I've grown to really care about you and Ian, and I don't want to avoid you anymore. It's been weighing on my mind."

"And making you hide from us?"

She twisted her lips in apology. "Yes, and I'm miserable." She uttered a little nonlaugh as if to punctuate her point.

Their gazes caught and held. "For the record, we've been miserable, too. And I'm listening," he said, never letting her hand go, holding it a little tighter to still the trembling. He could see her quickened pulse in the side of her neck and couldn't imagine what had her so frightened.

"It happened on prom night," she said, in a monotone. "The accident. We were…stupid, Drew. Kids being stupid. That's not an excuse— it's just what is."

"Okay."

She blew out a sigh. Tossed her hair. The pain on her face was plain. "We were drinking. It never should've happened like it did, but it happened. And now every time there's a prom- night accident in the country, the newspapers bring it up again, because we lost so many. It rips open that wound." She squeezed her eyes shut for a moment. "Over and over and over. Troublesome Gulch is to prom-night fatalities what Columbine is to school shootings."

"Wow. I had no idea." A beat passed. He didn't quite know how to ask, but he knew he had to. He cleared his throat. "Did everyone else…I mean, were you the only survivor?"

"Oh, no. No, I'm sorry. I thought you knew more about it than that."

"I don't know anything, Lex."

"Weird. Everyone knows everything in the Gulch, so I'm just used to that." She caressed his fingers gently with her own. "I figured you knew. You've been hanging out with Brody a bit, and…"

"I have, but he said it was your story to tell. And as for the grapevine, I'm not quite in the loop yet. I'm not much for gossip."

"You moved to the wrong town if that's the case," she said ruefully, before pressing her lips together. "Well, there were eight of us involved. The other survivors are Cagney, Erin…and Brody."

After a moment of shocked silence, he blew out a long breath. It made so much more sense that Brody had been so empathetic to him and Ian about their loss that day on the mountain. "All of you were there?"

"My best friends, yes. It's one of the reasons we've stayed so connected, and I'm so grateful to have them in my life. But there is always a hole where the others should've been. Mick, Randy, Kevin and Tad. Vibrant. Alive.

With families and futures. I think of them daily."

"I can imagine."

She stretched her neck side to side, as if to release an image from her mind. "It's taken a long time, Drew, but the town's healed. The survivors have, too, thank God. Everyone's managed to work through the pain."

He saw a soul-deep sadness in her eyes that made him want to hold her. "Everyone?" he asked softly.

The gaze that met his was steady, but she stayed quiet for a long time. Finally, she said, "Truth is, no. I haven't healed. Not completely, and I'm not talking about a spinal cord injury. I need to get it off my chest before we can be friends."

"Go ahead."

She looked as if she were bracing herself for a punch. "The accident was my fault."

His stomach dropped. Five simple words, but they'd obviously changed the course of Lexy's life forever. "What do you mean?"

"I mean, my fault. I caused it. It wouldn't have happened except for my irresponsibility." She paused, searched his face. "So, you see, my recklessness overshadows Gina's, by leaps and bounds. She may have killed herself, which is heartbreaking for you and Ian, and so…sad. But, me?" Her fingers went cold in his hands. "I killed four innocent kids. And that's never going away, Drew. Never."

Chapter Nine

Lexy's heart pounded in her chest as she waited for Drew to comment. To question. To say *something*. "Did you hear what I said?"

He rattled his head around in confusion. "Yes. Okay, back up. I'm trying to understand here, to not read into your words. What do you mean *exactly* when you say your *fault?* You were driving drunk?"

"No, no. My boyfriend was driving. And he wasn't even drinking that I remember, at least not like the rest of us." She looked at Drew and felt a sharp pang of regret. She knew there was no going back. The truth was out there, hanging between them like a thin sheet of glass, fragile and unsupported. Apt to shatter at any moment. She yearned to press her hand to that glass and have him do the same, to feel as if there were a way to connect. But Drew would likely realize exactly how much like Gina she was, exactly how poor a role model she would be for his son, and that would be it. So she didn't approach the glass. She just waited.

But once she'd learned how damaged he was by Gina's recklessness, she knew she had two choices. Walk away, or tell him everything, for her own peace of mind. The walking away hadn't worked. Now she had to give him a chance to run. Better now than after she became even more attached to him and Ian.

She'd tried walking away, and it hadn't worked. So now...

"If you weren't behind the wheel," he said carefully, "how could it possibly be your fault?"

She felt wild with wanting him to understand. "Because I...I was acting recklessly. Carrying on, distracting Randy."

He blinked. Twice. "Your boyfriend?"

She nodded, lips pressed together. She couldn't read him, and that was killing her. "I was climbing around the front of the SUV in that stupid, silky prom dress, and I slipped and knocked the steering wheel out of his hands. He tried to regain control, but he couldn't. Me. It was all me."

"But…it was an accident," he stated, more than asked.

"It was an accident I caused, that killed people, Drew," she said emphatically. "I was young and stupid and irresponsible. So…God, so irresponsible. But I knew better, and I did it anyway. Four lives cut short. Do you really want someone like that around your son?"

He searched her face. "Lexy…honey," he said slowly, "it was an accident."

She shook her head, denying that. "No. No excuses. I…know we haven't known each other that long, but for some reason, I don't want to hide that from you anymore. It's the worst thing I've ever done in my life. If we're going to be friends—"

"We *are* friends."

"Okay. Then. I couldn't give you less than the truth. Not after all you and Ian have been through. It's bothered me all month, ever since I learned how you felt about reckless behavior."

"So that was what I said? That I hated Gina's reckless behavior?"

She nodded.

"And that's why you didn't return any of my calls?"

"Yes. I'm sorry. That was cowardly. I didn't know what to do, and I was ashamed." She pushed out a frustrated sigh. "Ian paints me as some kind of a superhero simply because I answered a phone line, and—" Her words caught, and to her horror, her eyes filled with tears. "I'm nothing close to what Ian thinks of me. You're his father. An amazing father from what I've seen, who loves and protects him. If we're going to get to know each other—"

"And you'd like that?"

"Yes, I'd love that. You built a ramp," she said, with a teary laugh. "God, Drew, you…built a ramp."

He smiled. "I think you're going to like it."

"And I think you deserve to know what kind of person you're bringing into your little boy's life." He wasn't grasping the gravity of it all. "I'm not a hero, I'm not Ian's guardian angel, I don't look anything like a Disney princess, not that Disney would have me anyway, after what I've done, and—"

"Hey, now—"

"No," she slashed her hand in front of her. "I

take full responsibility for the devastation I've caused, Drew. Please know that. I've regretted that night every single day of my life, but that doesn't make it better. It never goes away. It will *never* go away. So, you see? My inability to walk? Small price to pay for the pure hell I set into motion."

Moments ticked by, punctuated by the utter silence of the training room.

Finally Drew leaned even closer. "Lexy," he said, seeming to measure his words, "look at me."

She did, through the wet veil of her lashes.

"Your ability to walk or not is irrelevant. To me. I'm unspeakably sorry about your friends, your boyfriend. About what you and the others have gone through. Truly, so sorry. You made a mistake, yes."

She dropped her gaze to their entwined hands. Here it came. She braced for the worst. To her surprise, he reached out and cupped her face in the safe circle of his palms. She lifted her watery eyes to look at him, breaking into a million pieces inside.

"But, all that said, who didn't make mistakes at that age?"

"There are mistakes, and then there are fatal mistakes."

"Look at what you've done with your life since."

A tear rolled down her cheek, and she lifted a hand to flick it away. "What? What I've done? I've worked a job—big deal. I've done what every other decent citizen in the world does, every day. The only difference is—and you need to really hear me—I'll have those deaths on my soul forever."

"I hear you." He chuckled, but with more sympathy than humor. "You've done far more than simply work a job, Lex. Are you always so incredibly hard on yourself?"

"Shouldn't I be?"

"No. You shouldn't be. I would be proud to have you as a role model in Ian's life. And that's saying a lot. Sometimes it's the people who go through the darkest of times that bring the most light."

She pressed her cheek into his palm, striving for composure. "All I wanted all these years, was for my friends to heal—"

"And they have, right?" He brushed his thumbs over her cheekbones, a gentle caress. "Brody, Cagney and Erin seem pretty happy to me."

His voice was way too level, too soothing. She couldn't succumb to that. "Yes, they are. Finally."

"And everything's okay at work?"

"Yes. I love my job, but I took it initially because I had a profound need to help people. To atone, or so I thought. But here it is, eleven years later. I've answered thousands of 9-1-1 calls, Drew, helped people like Ian. You. Sure, I've done that because I'm paid to do it, because it's a part of me. But none of it, not one save, not one call, has erased what I did all those years ago."

"It was a terrible tragedy, Lex, and you're right, nothing will erase it. But no one holds that against you…except you. What would you most want for the four friends you lost?"

"I'd want them to live. To have that chance."

"Don't you think they'd want the same for you?"

She blinked up at him, realizing, maybe for the first time, the truth of his words. Mick, Kevin, Tad and Randy wouldn't want her to turn her back on life because they'd died. In fact, doing so was an insult to their memories.

"Your situation isn't anything like Gina's. That would never have crossed my mind." He paused. "Don't you think you deserve to be happy now, too? Like the others?"

She sniffled as tears blurred her eyes. "I don't

know. I don't think I know how. I'm starting to…see your point."

"That's a good start."

She nodded. "I just needed to tell you. Everything. I want—no, I need you to explain to Ian I'm no superhero." Her voice grew more urgent. "Before he gets hurt all over again on my account. Please. I can't handle the pressure of the pedestal he's put me on."

"Okay. Lexy? Shh." He knelt on one knee in front of her chair and pulled her into an embrace, rubbing her back softly to soothe her. "Listen, whatever you need me to do, I'll do."

"Tell Ian I'm just a regular person, faults and all. I need you to tell him. Or there can never be anything between us, Drew. I don't want to live a lie."

Drew was rocked by all that Lexy had told him, not because he thought any less of her now than he ever had. Quite the opposite. He was struck more by the sheer depth of her torment and self-flagellation over a horrible mistake she'd made as a teenager. If he thought he'd been punishing himself over Gina's situation, over his anger about it, over his grief, Lexy had beat him by a mile.

She'd avoided him and Ian because she felt

unworthy? He never would've imagined that. "Lexy?" he said finally, "Nothing you've told me scares me away or makes you any less appealing. Nothing makes me not want you in our lives. Nothing is a deal breaker. Okay?"

"Okay."

He wanted to believe her. Yet, here she sat crying in the rehab room from pure shame, which he felt certain wasn't her style. But, damn, he had to say, she felt good in his arms. And he shouldn't be thinking along those lines at this moment, but she was so appealing. She squeezed him once and released him, sitting back. "I'm sorry. I'm not usually so emotional."

"I didn't think so. But this is tough."

"It's not just this. I've had a few surprises today."

He smiled at her. "Lex, do you want to get out of here? Go somewhere private so we can talk?"

Her eyes widened in surprise. "What?"

He stood and reached for her hand. "We can go to my house, hang out on the deck, eat ice cream. Ian would love to see you. Plus, I'd like for you to see the ramp. It's pretty awesome."

She paused for a moment, as if she were casting about for an excuse. "But, I haven't given you the grand tour of the rehab gym."

"It can wait."

She studied his face for several long moments, then reached out and shyly slid her palm into his. "Okay. Yes. I'd like that."

Stepping back, he assessed her. "You might want to, ah, splash your face or something."

Lexy peered into the full-length wall mirror with a horrified expression. "I look terrible!"

"Well, now, I don't think you're capable of that. But you do look as if you've been crying. The last thing you need is the grapevine buzzing that you left the hospital teary-eyed and holding hands with the new guy," he teased.

"God, no kidding. I should. I'll be right back."

While Lexy was in the ladies' locker room, Drew walked around the training room and inspected the state-of-the-art equipment. He'd love to have the opportunity to work with this kind of technology. Not many facilities had access to this kind of rehab equipment.

"Pretty amazing, isn't it?"

He spun to face Lexy, who'd emerged from the locker room mere moments after she'd left, fresh-faced. "Yeah. Jonas donated all this?"

She gazed around, taking in a deep breath and releasing it on a sigh. "All the high-tech stuff, yes. I feel so lucky. I can't tell you what a difference it's made in my training and stamina."

"I bet."

She peered up at him nervously. "Which… actually, before we leave, is something I hoped to talk to you about."

Drew cocked his head in confusion. "Your training or your stamina?" He waggled his eyebrows.

She laughed. "Training. My longtime rehab therapist and trainer, Kimberly, is leaving Troublesome Gulch to get married. Which is wonderful for her, but—"

"Not so great for you?"

"Exactly." Lexy pursed her lips in a pout. "I was such a baby about it when she told me this morning, but I'm going to miss her so much."

"I'm sorry, Lex."

"I know the hospital will put out feelers to fill her position, but it's difficult to get people who want to move way up here in the mountains."

He wished he could help. He could, but— He crossed toward Lexy and leaned his shoulder against a framed Universal weight stack. "Your free month at my gym is still open to you. Or longer. However long you need."

"I appreciate that. I do. My staff loves it there.

But, the thing is, my needs are a little different, Drew. I need to work out here. This is where all the equipment is."

"So, what are you suggesting?"

Lexy bit her bottom lip for a second, studying his face. "I know you're busy with your gym and Ian, but...would you consider training me? Just until they hire a new therapist?"

His chest clenched. The opportunity to spend tons of time with Lexy? It was a dream come true. "Really?"

Her face showed a bit of alarm. "Only if you want to. I don't want to take away from your own business." She worried her hands into a knot on her lap. "But I can't think of anyone else in town, Drew, and you were a coach."

Maybe he'd read too much into her request. "I see."

She groaned and smacked her fists on the armrests of her chair. "Okay, that's not the truth. I'm so not good at this...whatever it is you'd call what we're doing."

He smirked at her, bemused.

"I didn't think of anyone else in town, Drew. I wouldn't have asked anyone else. Not even Erin, who is—"

"Hardbody."

"Definitely. But I only thought of you. Not only are you qualified, but…I feel bad for how I've treated you and Ian, like we've lost a lot of time for—"

"Whatever it is you'd call what we're doing?" He really shouldn't tease her, but he couldn't help it. She was adorable flustered.

"Yes." She lifted her chin and squared her shoulders. "To be honest? I'd like to spend more time with you. With both of you. I want to get to know you and Ian better. If, you know, you're… up for that."

Was he ever. "I'd love to train you."

"Really?"

"Definitely."

For the first time that day, Lexy broke into a luminous smile, the kind he'd seen that night in the hospital. The sort of smile he could happily drown in.

She clasped her hands together. "That's great, Drew, seriously. I can't tell you how relieved I am."

Drew ran his fingers through his hair and glanced around. "I'll have to read up on some of the equipment. I've never trained someone with a spinal cord injury. You realize that, right?"

She touched her index finger to her bottom

lip, thinking. "Kimberly will be here for two more weeks, which is the exact amount of time left before the kick-off triathlon of the season. I'm sure she'd let you shadow her. She's an expert. She could show you the ropes."

"And I'm a quick study, so you've got yourself a deal."

"You think you could get me ready for the race?"

"I think I can set you up to win the race."

She laughed. "I've never won, Drew. I just like the exertion, the thrill of the chase. I'm okay not winning."

"Then prepare to be disappointed. I train winners."

That first step turned out to be the hardest. After a week, Drew had taken over most of Kimberly's duties, with Kimberly just supervising and giving suggestions. Lexy had never experienced such grueling workouts in her life. She loved it.

The morning of the race, she, Drew, Ian and all her friends gathered at the start point. The day was perfect for competition. Cool breeze, impeccable blue sky, electricity in the air. The lake water lapped with inviting regularity against the banks.

Drew squatted in front of her for a last-minute

pep talk. "Remember, Lex, go all out, but reserve energy for the final leg. That's going to make the difference between winning or not. Your swimming and cycling are strong enough that you should gain some time."

"Okay." Nervous anxiety had her rubbing her gloved palms together.

"Once you're in the water, all of us are going to book it down to the finish line to wait for you. Don't ever doubt that we're there, okay?"

"I won't."

His smile was languid, excited, beautiful to her. He looked at her as if he loved her. Which was absurd, really, but it was better than any energy drink. They'd trained hard; she wanted to make him proud.

"Daddy?" Ian asked.

They glanced toward the little boy, all slathered in sunscreen, his Troublesome Gulch baseball cap endearingly askew.

"Yeah, pal?"

"You gonna kiss Miss Lexy?"

Everyone within earshot laughed, and Ian peered around. "Just 'cuz, it looks like you want to."

"Come to think of it, son…"

Lexy's nervous energy ratcheted up as Drew's

gaze darkened, dropped to her lips. He moved closer…hesitated…studied her eyes for a moment, then captured her lips with his own.

Gentle, insistent. Right.

Lexy fought not to moan.

Before she drowned in it all, he pulled away. "Good luck, Lex. I believe in you."

"Thanks. I'll try not to let you down."

"Someday you'll realize that could never happen." He stood. "We'll be cheering you on at the end."

Lexy sat stunned as Ian, Drew and all her friends left the starting area. That kiss, a simple kiss, had awakened feelings inside her she hadn't even known existed anymore.

Rayna, her friend and fellow competitor, glided up. "Wow, Lex. What was that? More important, who was that?"

Lexy smiled at her longtime pal, a woman who understood everything about her physical condition more than any of her friends ever could, no matter how much they cared. "That was the man I think I'm falling in love with, Ray," she said.

Rayna laughed and gave her a high five. "It's about damn time, girl."

"I know." Lexy grinned. "Ready to do this?"

Rayna studied her dubiously. "I'm not sure. You're in better shape than I've ever seen you."

"Be afraid," Lexy teased. "Be very afraid. I plan to give you and everyone else some serious competition."

The swimming and biking segments of the race had gone beautifully, and Lexy felt fully energized for the finish. Part of it was knowing she'd put up better times than ever before. Part of it was her competitive spirit.

Part of it was knowing she'd see Drew at the end.

Somehow, the solitude of competing left her tons of time to think, and what she came up with was she wanted Drew. She wanted him. She'd even had the audacity to speak with her doctor the week before and found out that she could get pregnant if she so chose, although it wouldn't be without risks. But what was life without taking the good risks?

She saw the rainbow balloon arch in the distance and suddenly realized she could win this thing. Drew had been right. She didn't have to just participate in life anymore. She could win. That knowledge renewed the energy in her fatigued arms and she pumped the hand rims of her racing chair harder, knowing each spin carried her closer to winning.

Closer to Drew.

Closer to the possibility of having everything she had ever wanted in life...all those things she'd believed were no longer available to her.

The rainbow arch indicating the finish grew larger and larger, as did the cheers of the crowd. She was in the lead! Part of her wanted to glance back to see just how much of a lead she had, but Drew had warned her against that urge. Instead, she studied the arch and visualized the pot of gold on the other side. A man and a little boy with golden hair and open hearts. They wanted her in their lives. And dammit, she wanted to be in their lives.

Guilt or not.

Fear or not.

Walking or not.

She visualized the friends she'd lost...lovely Mick, sweet Randy, sincere Kevin and Tad, the boy they'd hardly gotten to know. She pictured them standing in the middle of the arch yelling and screaming for her to push. Push, Lexy. Harder. Harder. This one is for us.

Supercharged on love and adrenaline and everything that made life worth living, Lexy cranked it up even harder and single-mindedly aimed for that goal. Just get to that rainbow, Lex. Get there, and everything can change if you want it to.

Chapter Ten

Drew had never been so proud as he was seeing Lexy ramp things up for a strong finish. She'd never looked back, not once. And that was quite something for a woman who'd spent more than a decade not just glancing back, but staring back.

A strange squeeze started in his chest and left him tingly and stunned. At first he couldn't place it. But soon he realized it was love.

He loved Lexy.

She was the kindest, most determined, most beautiful woman he'd ever met in his life, and he wanted her *in* his life for the duration. He didn't care about any of the things that made her "different." In fact, he embraced them. But he wanted to move slowly, let her take the lead. He didn't want to do a single thing that might scare her away, because strangely enough, he didn't think he could face life without Lexy Cabrera. Not anymore. It was as though he'd been living in a windowless room since Gina's death, and Lexy had busted out the walls and brought in the sunshine.

He wasn't, by nature, a poetic guy. But that's how it felt.

A small hand slipped into his, and he glanced down at his son, similarly rapt. "I love her, Daddy."

Drew's throat tightened. He didn't want to speak his feelings, so he just squeezed Ian's hand, then lifted him to sit atop his shoulders.

"She's gonna win!" Ian said. "Those other people are way behind her."

"That's right. She is. Go big, or—"

"Go home," Ian finished.

Although this race was in White Peaks, the entire Gulch, it seemed, had turned out. Once she got close enough, the crowd caught on to the fact that one of Troublesome Gulch's beloved own was going to win this triathlon, and the excitement, the cheering, the pandemonium became deafening. When she got close enough, Drew could see the big grin on Lexy's face.

She knew it, too.

Other than the day Ian had received his Troublesome Gulch hero medal, Drew had never been so proud of someone in his life.

Lexy didn't bow under her challenges. She made the challenges part of her art, and damn, was she a beautiful picture.

She passed beneath the rainbow balloon arch amid a cacophony of cheers, moved out of the way and allowed herself to be enveloped by well-wishers. Erin handed her a bottle of water. Cagney, a towel. Faith had little Mickie in one arm and Erin's baby, Nate Jr., in the other, so she just danced around. The whole crowd seemed to be peppering Lexy with questions and congratulations, but Drew hung back, watched her down the bottle of water in one extended swallow. She wiped the moisture from her mouth with the back of her glove, and then her eyes sought the crowd.

They settled on him, and she smiled.

At that moment everyone disappeared. The world went silent. All he saw was Lexy, and he was pretty sure all she saw was him. At least, he hoped so.

The crowd must've seen it, too, because they parted, and she made her way toward him.

"Let me down, Daddy! Let me down!"

Drew squatted and allowed Ian to clamber off his shoulders. When Lexy was close enough, the little boy climbed up onto her lap. "You won, Miss Lexy!"

Though she snuggled the boy, her eyes never left Drew's. "I did win. Thanks to your daddy."

Drew remained squatted down and smiled into her face. "You did it."

"We did it," she corrected, her tone intimate.

"I'm so proud of you, Lex."

"Then kiss me again. And kiss me like you mean it."

Ian giggled and covered his face with both hands, and Drew tried to convey everything he felt in that warm, salty kiss. Because one thing he'd learned was that he *did* mean it.

After the race Drew and Lexy fell into a comfortable groove, and she felt stronger than ever and ready for the best racing season of her career.

Not only that, but they'd taken to spending a few evenings a week at her house or his, eating dinner, playing games with Ian, talking, getting to know one another like a regular, dating couple. And everything she learned about him made her fall a little harder. They hadn't shared any intimacy, beyond affectionate touches and lingering looks and the kisses on triathlon day, but she figured he was waiting for her to take the lead on that front. And she'd gotten to the point where she wanted to. Sure, she was scared, but one of them had to make the move.

The rest of their life was falling into place as if it had been fated. Sometimes she'd read to Ian before bed. Sometimes Drew would. Watching him snuggled against the headboard of the bed, Ian nestled against his side, both of them focused on an open book, was one of the most beautiful pictures she'd ever had in her mind.

So it was only natural that Lexy would head to Drew's house early to help him prepare for the housewarming two weeks after her big win. Not only were Brody, Faith, Erin, Nate, Nate's sister, Piper, who was in town, and Cagney and Jonas coming, along with their assorted kids, but many of the people Drew had met through the gym and the hero ceremony had been invited, as well. It would be a full house.

Drew was the self-proclaimed grill master, cooking burgers and brats, and Lexy had spent several days baking pies and cookies and other little bits of decadence. Everyone else had agreed to bring side dishes.

As Lexy set her last pie, rhubarb-strawberry, on the granite countertop to cool, she turned to face the great room and realized that somewhere along the way she'd begun to feel at home here. In this house, with this man and this boy. This felt like a housewarming for her, too, which made her tummy flutter and her heart expand.

Drew came in from the deck to retrieve a platter of meat from the fridge and stopped short. "Something smells good." He smiled, then crossed to the large refrigerator and pulled out a sheet pan of hamburger patties.

"Pie number ten," she said, angling her head toward the cooling dessert. "I got Ian down for a nap so he'll be ready to enjoy the festivities."

"What would I do without you?" Spontaneously Drew leaned down and kissed her lightly.

Her lips tingled from the unexpected contact. It emboldened her. She hadn't felt emotions like these in more than a decade. Or maybe never. All she knew was, she wanted more. She reached out and grabbed the front of his shirt, his face inches from hers. "Put that tray down," she said softly, but leaving no doubt that it wasn't a request.

She watched his expression deepen into something that made her squirm, then he put the tray on the island. "Lex—"

Pulling him closer, she hesitated just a moment, letting the heat of their breath mingle as their gazes clashed. He braced his palms on the armrests of her chair. She let her gaze drop languidly to his mouth, then pulled his lips to her own, thoroughly exploring them as she'd, frankly, never done before. But it seemed to come naturally with Drew.

Kneeling on one knee, he pulled her closer and threaded his fingers into her hair, moaning against her mouth as he deepened the kiss. His tongue explored hers, brash and wanting, until she pulled back and nipped his bottom lip. His eyes looked drunk with passion as he studied her.

"Have I ever thanked you?" she whispered against his lips. "For building the ramp? Training me? Letting me into your life with all my problems and complications?"

"I like your complications. And no," he said with a chuckle. "Not if that's the way you give thanks." He nipped at her lips again. "But feel free to thank me any time."

The whole mood was so intimate, so safe, Lexy

ran her finger in the hollow of Drew's throat. "So do you need to man the grill right now? Because I want to thank you…more thoroughly."

He froze momentarily, as if he couldn't believe his luck. Finally, around a swallow, he said, "Hell, no. Let it burn."

She laughed, but tingles danced beneath her skin. "Drew, I want you to know, I haven't… done this…since the accident. And I'm nervous."

"I understand, Lex."

"But…"

"Yes?"

"We have to discuss the logistics sometime. You need to know I'm perfectly capable of, well, making love. When the time comes. My condition doesn't affect that." She cut her gaze away, face blazing. "In fact, according to many of my SCI friends, while some nerves deaden, others are, I guess you'd say, heightened."

"Other nerves?"

"Um…internal ones."

His eyebrows rose. "Should we cancel the party?"

Lexy threw her head back and laughed. "No. I just had the feeling you might be uncertain about taking our relationship a step further."

"I prefer the word *deferential*."

"Either way. I just wanted you to know." She kissed him again. "I can, I will and I want to. But I'm scared."

Drew's expression softened, and he smoothed the backs of his fingers down her cheek. "Sweetheart, I would never do anything to scare you. And we can go as slowly as you want or need. But I can, I will and God, do I ever want to, too."

"You're not spooked by my condition?"

"Not in the least. You're the sexiest, most amazing woman I've met in…I can't tell you how long. You steal my breath, Lex. You scramble my brain. I'm all-in."

"Damn." A beat passed. "On second thought, maybe we *should* cancel the party."

They laughed and kissed, and kissed some more, and Lexy felt more alive than she had in years. Her skin sizzled and her heart bloomed. But pretty soon it was time for guests to begin ringing that doorbell. Regretfully, Drew went back out to the grill, while Lexy set up a buffet of sorts on the dining table and island, then rushed down the hallway to wake up Ian.

The little guy was still out cold, cherubic in slumber. She approached his bed and just watched him, astonished by the perfection of this child. She loved him. The realization was like a backhand smack across the cheek that left her stinging. She loved this little boy with her whole heart and soul, and it had probably started the day they had connected over the phone line.

Please let me be good enough for him.

"Hey, little man," she said, her tone gentle. "Time for the party. Ian?"

His eyes fluttered open. "Is everyone here, Mommy?" he murmured, rubbing his fists in his eyes.

Lexy was rendered speechless by his words. Clearly it was the sleep talking, but that didn't detract from the realization that…she wanted this. She wanted family and potlucks, kisses in the kitchen and stories at bedtime. Whispered promises and private glances. She wanted a full life, and she wanted it with Drew and Ian. She wanted Ian to be comfortable calling her Mommy.

Sleepy and warm, Ian crawled into her lap and snuggled against her shoulder. She cupped his head, brushing back his omnipresent cowlicks. "Did you sleep well?"

He nodded against her body. "Miss Lexy?"

"Yes, baby?"

"Do you wanna be my mommy?"

Lexy's stomach plunged like a snapped bungee cord. "Ian, sweetheart, you have a mommy already."

"But she's in heaven."

"I know."

He nestled closer. "I want you to be my earth mommy. Don't you love us enough?"

If a person could feel a heart crack, Lexy just had. But she couldn't make childlike promises that came with adult concerns. "Oh, honey." She kissed the top of his head. "Of course I love you. I'll always be here for you."

"But I want a mommy."

"I know."

"And brothers and sisters."

Thud.

She'd put it out of her head that Drew and Gina had planned a large family, but it popped back up like a leering jack-in-the-box, reminding her that she was lacking in one important area. She didn't know what to say, how to handle such an awkward line of questioning. Yes, her doctor had told Lexy she could become pregnant, but also that it might leave her more disabled. There were a lot of unknowns. "How about we get ready for the party and talk about this later?" she said, patting his back.

"Okay." He kissed her on the cheek. "I love

you, Miss Lexy. Mommy." And with that, he jumped off her lap and bounded toward the restroom to brush his teeth, change his clothes and make a futile attempt at taming his hair.

Lexy, however, sat immobile, in a mixture of worry and wanting.

Chapter Eleven

The housewarming party was a rousing success, and Lexy was able to put Ian's comments about wanting siblings out of her head and enjoy it. At least for a while. After the pie had been eaten, and everyone had said their goodbyes, Ian climbed off her lap—where he'd spent most of the day—and let his father carry him to bed.

And it all came back. They needed to discuss it.

Lexy stared up at the star-strewn sky, enjoying the heat from the fire in the chimenea. Was she just fooling herself here? Drumming up dreams that could never come to fruition? No matter how much she adored Ian and Drew, the wrong puzzle piece could never complete a perfect picture. And their life was a perfect picture minus that one piece: a mommy who could absolutely provide a house full of brothers and sisters, a gigantic, loving household.

Fact: Drew wanted a large family.

Fact: Ian wanted siblings.

Fact: Lexy wasn't one-hundred-percent sure she was the woman who could provide either of those things. So what was she doing, getting herself more and more tangled up with a fantasy that could never come true? Playing with danger? She'd given that up long ago. Yes, she wanted Drew with a ferocity that surprised her, but she was also scared. She'd lingered after everyone else had left so she could talk to Drew. Talk things out. Figure out exactly what they were doing and why.

She yearned for the laughter and party sounds that had swirled around her, distracting her from the bleak thoughts in her head. But now, in the silence, she'd lost her festive vibe. She sighed.

As if sensing her need, Drew stepped out onto the deck and pulled up a deck chair next to her. "Ian is out like a light. Didn't even make it through a single book."

"It was a big day for him," she said.

"Everything okay, Lex?"

She gave him a winsome smile, appreciating the feel of the cool evening breeze flowing through her hair. "Yeah."

He reached for her hand. She let him.

"It was a great party," she said. When all else fails? Small talk. "If this house isn't warmed by now, I don't know what would make it warmer."

"I do," he said, capturing her gaze in his. He rubbed her hand between his palms and looked at her with so much adoration, it was difficult for Lexy to grasp. He lifted her hand and kissed the back of it. "Lexy, that kiss we shared earlier today? It awakened something inside me. It gave me hope."

Her throat tightened with the sheer pain of it all. "Drew…we need to talk about that."

His expression sobered immediately. "Okay."

"Ian called me Mommy," she blurted, and heat immediately spread up her neck and flamed her cheeks. "Earlier, I mean. When I got him up for the party."

"Ah," Drew said, as if that explained it all. "Okay."

"At first I thought it was because he was half-asleep, but then he told me…he wanted me to *be* his mommy."

"Well, that's kind of his thing these days."

"I know. But…he sounded serious this time. And he also said…" Her chest hurt. She twisted her mouth to the side, wondering if she should even bring any of this up to Drew. Ian was a six-year-old. What did it matter?

"What? You can tell me."

She adjusted the skirt of her sundress over her legs. "He said he wanted a baby brother or sister. I'm sorry."

A beat passed, then Drew said, "No, I'm sorry" with a sigh. "He's just a little boy, Lex."

"I know. But he's confused."

"About what?"

"Us," she said after a moment of considering it. "The thought of disappointing him kills me. There is a possibility I could become pregnant, if…if it got to that point. But it could also change things for me physically. I don't know if the risk is worth it."

"I'd never want to make things more difficult for you, Lex. So what do you suggest?"

"Maybe we need to make our relationship more clear to him. Or…maybe we need to spend time apart." A strand of hair blew across her face, and Drew reached up and smoothed it behind her ear.

"You want to spend time apart?"

A beat passed. She chuckled softly. "No. Just the opposite."

"Well, good. Neither do I." He kissed her hand again. "And frankly, I'm not sure why Ian calling you Mommy would bother you so much. It's obvious how much you adore my son."

"I do. I love him." She sighed. "But, I'm not his mother, Drew. Gina is his mother."

"I think he understands the difference, as much as a six-year-old can. What exactly would you like me to say to him about our relationship?" Drew asked, in a tone both rough and silky.

Lexy desperately wished she could pretend they were a couple, that they had a future. There was an attraction, sure. But the large family thing hung over her head. She didn't know if Drew had any interest in adopting. Hell, she didn't know how she felt about any of it, either. What she did know was she needed more time to figure it all out. "The truth, I guess."

"That's what I'm asking. What's the truth?"

Lexy searched his face, feeling a loss. "I don't know. Tell him we're friends."

He watched her for a good, long time. "What about our discussion earlier? About…making love."

Her smile came gradually, but the visceral reaction inside her happened much quicker. "Okay, tell him we're very *good* friends."

Drew laughed softly. "Lex, honey, I'm asking you to tell me what you want."

"What do you mean, exactly?"

"From this. From our relationship?"

Everything. All of it. Family. Hiking trips.

But you can't have it, Lexy. You don't deserve it.

Yes, you do.

If Drew had taught her anything, it was that she deserved everything she wanted in this life. And she wanted him.

She blew out a miserable sigh and glanced out over the mountain range. "This is…all new for me. Other than a high-school romance, I've never…" She cast him a sidelong glance. "Do you understand?"

Drew hung his head for so long, Lexy worried he might be angry. At last he looked up. "I do. But I want you to know where I'm coming from, too."

She swallowed thickly. "Okay."

"I've been sleepwalking through life since Gina's death. Hell, long before that." He scrubbed a hand through his hair. "You make me feel alive, Lexy."

"I feel the same. But…" She shook her head, filled with emotion.

"But what?"

"I can't provide you with the large family you planned on having, Drew."

"You don't want a family?"

"It's not that. I always planned on having a family…before. But I don't know that I could provide you with even one child."

Drew cupped her face in his hands, as if she were a precious thing. "Do you think I care about that? That I'd ask you to become pregnant and compromise your own health?"

"You said you wanted a large family."

"I said Gina and I had planned on a large family, but you know what? Gina also planned on seeing her thirtieth birthday."

"Of course," she whispered.

Drew kissed her and pulled his hands away. "Lex, you know probably better than anyone that life can change in an instant. My life changed the day Ian was born. It changed the day Gina died. And, honey, it changed most dramatically the day I met you."

Tears came to her eyes, and she bit on the insides of her cheeks to keep steady.

"I love you, Lexy," he whispered. "I've never met a woman like you, and I've never wanted someone in my son's life as much as I want you here."

Her emotions bubbled over, and a single tear ran down her face. "I may never walk again. And, Drew, I like me for me. I'm okay with that."

He kissed the tear away. "I'm okay with that, too."

"And if I can't have children—"

"Then Ian will be the luckiest only child in the world, with a father who loves him, a mother who's his guardian angel and an earth mommy who's the best role model I could possibly want."

"Drew?"

"Yes, honey?"

"Ian's asleep?"

"Definitely."

She swallowed past a shaky throat. "I trust you."

He smiled. "I'm glad."

"But I'm still scared."

"I understand that, too."

She reached her arms up to him. "Make love to me, Drew. Please."

He didn't hesitate for a moment. Bending so

Lexy could put her arms around his neck, he lifted her gently and carried her inside, their lips touching, pulling back, touching again.

In the bedroom Drew placed her gently on the bed and followed her down, covering her body with his own. She inhaled the summer-sunshine smell of him and gave as good as she got with her mouth, her whispers, her hands. Drew reached over his shoulder and pulled his polo shirt over his head, then slowly slid Lexy's sundress up her body and over her head.

For a moment she felt shy.

"God, you're beautiful," he said, before kissing his way down to her full breasts. Her nipples tightened with an almost painful sweetness against his tongue, and a sense of fulfillment so effervescent consumed her that she laughed.

Drew peered up at her in the low lamplight and smiled. "Well, that's not the reaction I expected."

"I'm sorry. I'm just so happy I met you."

"And to think you might not have if not for—"

"Smart little Ian, remembering to call 9-1-1," Lexy said, releasing the past, embracing the future and giving in to the moment. "My precious little matchmaker."

* * * * *

ALEXANDROS KAREDES, SNOW DUSTING the shoulders of his leather jacket and glittering like jewels in his dark hair, stood at the door. Maria felt the blood drain from her head.

"Good evening, Ms. Santos."

His voice was as she remembered it. Deep. Husky. Perfect English, but with the faintest hint of a Greek accent. And cold, as cold as it had been that awful morning she would never forget, when he'd accused her of horrible things, called her terrible names....

"Aren't you going to ask me in?"

She fought for composure. Last time they'd faced each other, they'd been on his turf. Now they were on hers. She was in command here, and that meant everything.

"There's a sign on the door downstairs," she said, her tone every bit as frigid as his. "It says No Soliciting or Vagrants."

His lips drew back in a wolfish grin. "Very amusing."

"What do you want, Prince Alexandros?"

A tight smile eased across his mouth and it killed her that even now, knowing he was a vicious, arrogant man, she couldn't help but notice what a handsome mouth it was. Chiseled. Generous. Beautiful, like the rest of him, which made him living proof that beauty could, indeed, be only skin deep.

"Such formality, Maria. You were hardly so proper the last time we were together."

She knew his choice of words was deliberate. She felt her face heat; she couldn't help that but she damned well didn't have to let him lure her into a verbal sparring match.

"I'll ask you once more, your highness. What do you want?"

"Ask me in and I'll tell you."

"I have no intention of asking you in. Tell me

why you're here or don't. It's your choice, just as it will be my choice to shut the door in your face."

He laughed. It infuriated her but she could hardly blame him. He was tall—six-two, six-three—and though he stood with one shoulder leaning against the door frame, hands tucked casually into the pockets of the jacket, his pose was deceptive. He was strong, with the leanly muscled body of a well-trained athlete.

She remembered his body with painful clarity. The feel of him under her hands. The power of him moving over her. The taste of him on her tongue.

Suddenly, he straightened, his laughter gone. "I have not come this distance to stand in your doorway," he said coldly, "and I am not going to leave until I am ready to do so. I suggest you stand aside and stop behaving like a petulant child."

A petulant child? Was that what he thought? This man who had spent hours making love to her and had then accused her of—of trading her body for profit?

Except it had not been love, it had been sex. And the sooner she got rid of him, the better.

She let go of the doorknob and stepped aside. "You have five minutes."

He strolled past her, bringing cold air and the scent of the night with him. She swung toward him, arms folded. He reached past her, pushed the door closed, then folded his arms, too. She wanted to open the door again but she'd be damned if she was going to get into a who's-in-charge-here argument with him. She was in charge, and he would surely see a tussle over the ground rules as a sign of weakness.

Instead, she looked past him at the big clock above her work table.

"Ten seconds gone," she said briskly. "You're wasting time, your highness."

"What I have to say will take longer than five minutes."

"Then you'll just have to learn to economize. More than five minutes, I'll call the police."

Instantly, his hand was wrapped around her wrist. He tugged her toward him, his dark-chocolate eyes almost black with anger.

"You do that and I'll tell every tabloid shark I can contact about how Maria Santos tried to buy a five-hundred-thousand-dollar commission by seducing a prince." He smiled thinly. "They'll lap it up."

* * * * *

What will it take for this billionaire prince to realize he's falling in love with his mistress…?
Look for
BILLIONAIRE PRINCE, PREGNANT MISTRESS
by Sandra Marton.
Available July 2009 from
Harlequin Presents®.

We'll be spotlighting a different series every month throughout 2009 to celebrate our 60th anniversary.

Look for Harlequin® Presents in July!

TWO CROWNS, TWO ISLANDS, ONE LEGACY

A royal family, torn apart by pride and its lust for power, reunited by purity and passion

Step into the world of Karedes
beginning this July with

BILLIONAIRE PRINCE, PREGNANT MISTRESS
by
Sandra Marton

Eight volumes to collect and treasure!

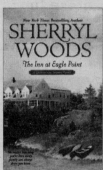

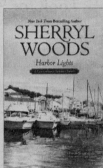

THE BELLES OF TEXAS

They're as strong as the state that raised
them. The Belle sisters aren't afraid to go
after what they want, whether it's reclaiming
their ranch or their family.

Linda Warren
CAITLYN'S PRIZE

Thanks to her deceased father's gambling
debts, Caitlyn Belle's beloved High Five Ranch
is in dire straits. Particularly because the
will stipulates that if the ranch doesn't turn
a profit in six months, it must be sold to
Judd Calhoun—the man Caitlyn jilted
fourteen years ago. And Cait knows Judd has
been waiting a long time for his revenge....

*Look for the first book
in The Belles of Texas miniseries,
on sale in July wherever books are sold.*

You're invited to join our Tell Harlequin Reader Panel!

By joining our new reader panel you will:

- Receive Harlequin® books—they are FREE and yours to keep with no obligation to purchase anything!
- Participate in fun online surveys
- Exchange opinions and ideas with women just like you
- Have a say in our new book ideas and help us publish the best in women's fiction

In addition, you will have a chance to win great prizes and receive special gifts! See Web site for details. Some conditions apply. Space is limited.

To join, visit us at
www.TellHarlequin.com.

REQUEST YOUR FREE BOOKS!

2 FREE NOVELS PLUS 2 FREE GIFTS!

SPECIAL EDITION®

Life, Love and Family!

YES! Please send me 2 FREE Silhouette Special Edition® novels and my 2 FREE gifts (gifts are worth about $10). After receiving them, if I don't wish to receive any more books, I can return the shipping statement marked "cancel." If I don't cancel, I will receive 6 brand-new novels every month and be billed just $4.24 per book in the U.S. or $4.99 per book in Canada. That's a savings of at least 15% off the cover price! It's quite a bargain! Shipping and handling is just 50¢ per book.* I understand that accepting the 2 free books and gifts places me under no obligation to buy anything. I can always return a shipment and cancel at any time. Even if I never buy another book from Silhouette, the two free books and gifts are mine to keep forever.

235 SDN EYN4   335 SDN EYPG

Name _____ (PLEASE PRINT) _____

Address _____ Apt. # _____

City _____ State/Prov. _____ Zip/Postal Code _____

Signature (if under 18, a parent or guardian must sign)

Mail to the **Silhouette Reader Service:**
IN U.S.A.: P.O. Box 1867, Buffalo, NY 14240-1867
IN CANADA: P.O. Box 609, Fort Erie, Ontario L2A 5X3

Not valid to current subscribers of Silhouette Special Edition books.

Want to try two free books from another line?
Call 1-800-873-8635 or visit www.morefreebooks.com.

* Terms and prices subject to change without notice. Prices do not include applicable taxes. Sales tax applicable in N.Y. Canadian residents will be charged applicable provincial taxes and GST. Offer not valid in Quebec. This offer is limited to one order per household. All orders subject to approval. Credit or debit balances in a customer's account(s) may be offset by any other outstanding balance owed by or to the customer. Please allow 4 to 6 weeks for delivery. Offer available while quantities last.

Your Privacy: Silhouette is committed to protecting your privacy. Our Privacy Policy is available online at www.eHarlequin.com or upon request from the Reader Service. From time to time we make our lists of customers available to reputable third parties who may have a product or service of interest to you. If you would prefer we not share your name and address, please check here. ☐

SSE09R

Stay up-to-date on all your romance reading news!

The Inside Romance newsletter is a **FREE** quarterly newsletter highlighting our upcoming series releases and promotions!

Go to
eHarlequin.com/InsideRomance
or e-mail us at
InsideRomance@Harlequin.com
to sign up to receive
your **FREE** newsletter today!

You can also subscribe by writing to us at: HARLEQUIN BOOKS
Attention: Customer Service Department
P.O. Box 9057, Buffalo, NY 14269-9057

Please allow 4-6 weeks for delivery of the first issue by mail.

IRNBPA0109

 *Silhouette*®

COMING NEXT MONTH
Available June 30, 2009

#1981 THE TEXAS BILLIONAIRE'S BRIDE—Crystal Green
The Foleys and the McCords
For Vegas showgirl turned nanny Melanie Grandy, caring for the
daughter of gruff billionaire Zane Foley was the perfect gig…until
she fell for him, and her secret past threatened to bring down the
curtain on her newfound happiness.

#1982 THE DOCTOR'S SECRET BABY—Teresa Southwick
Men of Mercy Medical
It was no secret that Emily Summers had shared a night of passion
with commitment-phobe Dr. Cal Westen. But she kept him in the
dark when she had their child. Would a crisis bring them together as
a family…for good?

#1983 THE 39-YEAR-OLD VIRGIN—Marie Ferrarella
It wasn't easy when Claire Santaniello had to leave the convent to
teach and take care of her sick mother. Luckily, widowed father and
vice detective Caleb McClain was there for her as she found her way
in the world…and into his arms.

#1984 HIS BROTHER'S BRIDE-TO-BE—Patricia Kay
Jill Jordan Emerson was engaged to a wealthy businessman several
years her senior—until she came face-to-face with his younger
brother Stephen Wells, a.k.a. the long-lost father of her son! Now
which brother would claim this bride-to-be as his own?

#1985 LONE STAR DADDY—Stella Bagwell
Men of the West
It was a simple case of illegal cattle trafficking on a New Mexico
ranch, and Ranger Jonas Redman thought he had the assignment
under control—until the ranch's very single, very pregnant heiress
Alexa Cantrell captured his attention and wouldn't let go….

#1986 YOUR RANCH OR MINE?—Cindy Kirk
Meet Me in Montana
When designer Anna Anderssen came home to Sweet River, she
should have known she'd run right into neighboring rancher Mitchell
Donovan, the one man who could expose the secrets—and reignite
passions—that made her run in the first place!

SSECNMBPA0609

SPECIAL EDITION